"You think—" _for emphasis_ "—you have all the answers. You think—" another poke "—you know what's best for my son. You think—"

Nelson grabbed her finger, holding it prisoner. "I may not know what's best for Seth, but I sure as hell know when a boy needs discipline."

She gasped. "How dare—"

"I dare because it's obvious that you're barely making ends meet. That you're working yourself to death while your kid sits on his butt, talking on the phone to his friends."

Ellen's eyes burned. "Are you through insulting me?"

He released her finger and raked a hand through his hair. "I have a lot of experience running a business. I can help you get this farm back on solid financial ground and keep an eye on your boy at the same time."

"Besides the fact that I don't approve of the way you deal with my son, do you honestly think I'd trust a man who doesn't know one end of a cow from another to handle my finances?"

"I don't see that you have much of a choice."

Dear Reader,

I cherish the childhood memories of my Grandpa Bud taking me and my brother, Brett, on Sunday-afternoon drives along the rural roads of southern Wisconsin. I'd stare out the car window at the passing farms, count the silos and watch the cows line up outside the milking barns, all the while dreaming of what life would be like if I'd grown up on a farm.

I've always had a soft spot in my heart for farmers. Farming is an exhausting, demanding profession that brings out the best and worst in people. With the changing economy, global warming and a host of other obstacles, farmers today often face an uncertain future—like the heroine in this story. Although I have a feeling Ellen Tanner just might meet with a happy ending....

If you would like to read the first book of my MCKADE BROTHERS series, *Aaron Under Construction*, you can still get it through online retailers. And don't miss Ryan's story, the final book of the series, coming in August 2007.

I love to hear from readers, so please visit me at www.marinthomas.com or e-mail me at marin@marinthomas.com.

Happy reading!

Marin

Nelson In Command
MARIN THOMAS

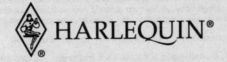

HARLEQUIN®

TORONTO • NEW YORK • LONDON
AMSTERDAM • PARIS • SYDNEY • HAMBURG
STOCKHOLM • ATHENS • TOKYO • MILAN • MADRID
PRAGUE • WARSAW • BUDAPEST • AUCKLAND

ISBN-13: 978-0-373-75152-5
ISBN-10:   0-373-75152-4

NELSON IN COMMAND

Copyright © 2007 by Brenda Smith-Beagley.

ABOUT THE AUTHOR

Typical of small-town kids, all Marin Thomas, born in Janesville, Wisconsin, could think about was how to leave after she graduated from high school.

Her six-foot-one-inch height was her ticket out. She accepted a basketball scholarship at the University of Missouri in Columbia, where she studied journalism. After two years she transferred to U of A at Tucson, where she played center for the Lady Wildcats. While at Arizona, she developed an interest in fiction writing and obtained a B.A. in radio-television. Marin was inducted in May 2005 into the Janesville Sports Hall of Fame for her basketball accomplishments.

Her husband's career in public relations has taken them to Arizona, California, New Jersey, Colorado, Texas and Illinois, where she currently calls Chicago her home. Marin can now boast that she's seen what's "out there." Amazingly enough, she's a living testament to the old adage "You can take the girl out of the small town, but you can't take the small town out of the girl." Her heart still lies in small-town life, which she loves to write about in her books.

Books by Marin Thomas

HARLEQUIN AMERICAN ROMANCE
1024—THE COWBOY AND THE BRIDE
1050—DADDY BY CHOICE
1079—HOMEWARD BOUND
1124—AARON UNDER CONSTRUCTION†

†The McKade Brothers

To Harry and Sue Amen.

I will never forget the first time my family visited your farm in Colorado. I thought for sure I'd landed in a never-ending episode of *Green Acres*. A one-legged chicken. A thirteen-year-old cousin who drove a pickup like a bat out of hell. The train that rattled your house when it blew past the front yard. The practical jokes you coaxed us kids to play on my parents—remember peanut butter on the bedsheets? And my introduction to a corn boil… who'd ever have thought that partying with a bunch of farmers could be so much fun!

I remember my throat aching and tears burning my eyes as our family waved goodbye and drove back home to Wisconsin. A part of me yearned to stay on the farm, where the days were long, the work grueling, the income uncertain, but the love and laughter abundant.

I wish the world were full of people like you, Harry and Sue. People who live life to the fullest, laugh a lot and love much. You're the salt of the earth and I feel blessed to be a part of your family.

Chapter One

What the…?

Nelson McKade slammed his foot against the brake of his Jaguar XKR Coupe, praying the Brembo brand lived up to its claim of incredible stopping power. If the front bumper so much as nudged the supersized hog twenty feet ahead, he'd return the luxury car to the dealership and demand his 84,000 dollars back.

In a matter of seconds the vehicle squealed to a jarring halt inches from the massive roadblock. Dumbfounded, he stared out the windshield at the pig whose head and upper body reached above the hood of the car. What the heck were farmers feeding these animals—humans?

One by one he pried his fingers from the steering wheel, then glanced in the rearview mirror. Black rubber tire marks—in two perfectly straight lines—scarred the road. He stepped out of the car and surveyed the party of swine milling in the middle of RR 7.

If he hadn't been studying the atlas when he'd sped around the curve, he would have had plenty of time to brake. In Ireland a driver expected herds of sheep to cross roads, but who the hell knew Illinois farmers herded pigs the same way?

Shielding his eyes from the early-June afternoon sun, he searched the area for the pig herder. The hog near his bumper *oinked,* scaring the crap out of him. "Shoo!" He waved a hand in the air, but the fat piece of lard wouldn't budge. A moment later, snot spewed from the snout, spraying the hood of the car. Then the animal leaned in and scratched its smelly, filthy, dingy pink flank against the grill.

"Knock it off!"

The beast snorted, then strolled away to join the others lounging in the gully alongside the road.

"Suuu-eee! Suuu-eee!"

Swiveling in the direction of the sound, Nelson focused on a dirt path across the road. The snap of broken branches grew louder. A moment later a man emerged from the wooded area. *Farmer Brown.* Complete with a John Deere cap, baggy overalls and a shotgun slung over one shoulder.

"Blast it all, Homer! Git yer fat bacon arse through that gate!"

Homer? Nelson spotted the hog he'd almost flattened, and sure enough, the animal's ears perked at his owner's command.

"I oughtta fry yer hide…." The threat trailed off when the farmer noticed Nelson. After a brief hesitation, he grumbled, "Homer, you done pissed me off real good this time," then offered Nelson, "Sorry 'bout my pigs, mister. Most times no one uses this road."

Nelson pointed to the massive hog. "Homer?"

"Yep." The man's chest puffed up. "Fattest hog in Pritchard County. Took first place last year at the 4-H fair."

Nelson didn't know much about 4-H fairs or pigs, but weren't the winning animals usually sold for top dollar?

"Didn't have the heart to auction Homer off," the man answered, reading Nelson's thoughts. "Homer done saved the day when he was nothing but a squirt. He come a chargin' through the doggie door on the back porch, squealin' up a storm. Led me to a pile of smolderin' hay. I coulda lost the whole barn if the hay'd caught fire."

"Smart pig," Nelson mumbled, suspicious of the far-fetched story.

"Name's Becker. Bill Becker." The farmer offered his hand.

"Nelson McKade." He tried not to think about where that hand had been all morning. "You wouldn't happen to know if the Tanner farm is nearby?"

"Which Tanners you lookin' for?"

"There's more than one Tanner family?"

"Yes, sir. There's the Tanners of Kentucky and the Tanners of Illinois."

This guy was a nutcase. "I'm searching for the Illinois Tanners."

"Well, then you got a bit o' problem. This here's Kentucky."

"Kentucky? Wait a minute." Nelson leaned through the open car window and snatched the atlas off the passenger seat. He pointed to a black dot on the map of Illinois. "Four Corners is right here on RR 7."

"Yes, sir, but the road forks off a ways back."

Positive there had been no marker warning of a split in the road, Nelson insisted, "I didn't see any sign."

Farmer Becker guffawed. "Ain't surprised. Tornado o' '72 blew it down. Ain't never been stuck back in the ground."

Nelson had entered the twilight zone. He checked his watch. It was already three in the afternoon, and he hadn't eaten lunch. "How far back is the junction?"

"'Bout thirty-five miles." The farmer stuck his fingers in his mouth and whistled. When Homer twisted his massive head, his owner spat a stream of tobacco juice across the hood of the car, and the hog caught the glob of spit in his snout, then squealed. "Taught him that trick," the farmer chortled.

Oh, my God.

"Say, you wouldn't mind givin' me a hand with Homer, would ya?"

The hog lay on his side, watching the other pigs pass single file through an opening in the fence. "What kind of help?"

"Homer's so danged fat I gots to shove his arse through the gate or he gits wedged in."

Being on the *arse* end of Homer had about as much appeal as reviewing executive expense accounts.

"The sooner I gits him into the field, the sooner I git back to Mary."

"Mary?"

"Mary's my wife. She's havin' a hissy fit 'cause I forgot it's her birthday. Danged woman's turnin' fifty." The farmer headed for Homer, grumbling, "Looks more like seventy."

For a minute Nelson watched the man struggle to coax the hog up on to his short legs. A few kicks to the massive rump and Homer grunted, then got to his feet. The farmer led the pig to the gate, and sure enough, the hog got halfway through the opening, then got stuck.

Oh, hell. Nelson studied his white dress shirt and just-from-the-cleaners slacks. He'd already removed his tie and suit jacket after a morning meeting with his corporate executives. He should have changed into jeans and a T-shirt in his office before leaving Chicago on his grandfather's stupid quest, but he had wanted to hit the road before traffic got bad on the Dan Ryan Expressway. He headed for the ditch.

"Shove his arse."

Homer's *arse* would put the fat lady in the circus to shame. Nelson edged closer, got a whiff of something nasty and gagged. Holding his breath, he set one hand on either side of the hog's corkscrew tail.

"On the count o' three." Farmer Becker hopped over the fence into the field, then moved in front of the animal and grabbed the pig's ears. "One, two, three."

Nelson shoved, sought purchase with his leather dress shoes and shoved again. Pressed his shoulder to the animal's rump and shoved, shoved, shoved. Nothing. The stupid beast hadn't budged. Breathing heavily—too heavily for a thirty-seven-year-old man who worked out daily in the corporate gym—he cursed.

"Well, shucks. I ain't brought the hogs to this here pasture in over two months. Didn't think Homer'd gained that much weight."

"How much does Homer weigh?" Nelson huffed.

"Last time I checked, he was eight hundred and ten pounds."

Eight hundred and ten pounds?

The farmer scrambled across the fence and joined Nelson behind the hog. "On the count—"

"I know. Three."

This time, two shoulders pushed the massive arse. Nelson felt the animal slide forward a good foot. "Can he make it the rest of the way?" he grunted.

"Might." The farmer—who was hardly breathing heavy, Nelson noticed with disgust—scrambled over the fence again and removed what appeared to be a dog biscuit from the front pocket of his overalls. "Treat, Homer?"

The hog's tail twitched and his ears waggled.

As the farmer waved the bone in front of the pink snout, Nelson rammed Homer's butt with all his might. The animal lunged forward and Nelson lost his balance, landing on the ground in a tangle of thistle and weeds. Scrambling to get out of the way of flying hog hooves, he managed to avoid a kick in the head, but wasn't fast enough to duck the brown glob that squirted from Homer's rear and splattered the front of his dress shirt.

"Crap!" Nelson's nose curled at the stinky, wet warmth soaking the material.

"Ouwee, mister. You scared the poop right out o' Homer. He ain't never done that 'afore."

Swearing he'd make his grandfather pay, Nelson crawled to his feet. *Acquiescence, my ass.* He'd followed someone else's order—and look where that had gotten him—covered in pig manure. "The damn hog deserves a trip to the slaughterhouse."

"No, sirree. I'm enterin' him in the fattest-pig competition at the end of the summer." He swatted Homer's flank and the tub of lard ambled off to join his friends devouring the crop in the field. Farmer Becker tipped his cap. "Thanks for the help, mister. Watch for a dead tree. The road forks there."

Nelson removed his dress shirt and his white undershirt, rolled them in a ball, then stuffed them into the far corner of the trunk. He rummaged through his luggage, found a bottle of cologne and squirted several shots at his chest to cover *l'odeur de swine* lingering on him. Then he donned a golf shirt and tucked the tails into his suit slacks. Not the outfit he'd planned to wear the first time he met his new boss, but what the heck. He was probably overdressed for a farm hand, anyhow.

After making a U-turn, he waved to the farmer and drove northeast toward the Illinois border. Thirty-five miles…plenty of time to consider different ways he'd make his grandfather pay for this foolish *life lesson* he demanded Nelson learn.

Acquiescence. Where in the heck did his ninety-one-year-old grandfather dream up this stuff? After the loss of Nelson's parents in a plane crash, his grandfather had raised him and his two brothers, Ryan and Aaron, since they were toddlers. But that didn't give the old man the right to lord over his grown grandsons forever.

Then why are you doing this? Nelson asked himself. *You could have easily refused.*

The temptation to do just that had eaten at him for days. But he had great respect for his grandfather. Patrick McKade had learned the import-export business from his own father and had expanded the family's holdings. After Nelson had graduated from Harvard Business School, he'd spent two years under his grandfather's tutelage before taking over the helm of the company at age twenty-four.

In truth, Nelson had a natural ability when it came to running a company and he enjoyed the challenge of growing a business. That, along with the need to make his grandfather proud of him, drove Nelson to succeed. By the time he'd celebrated thirty years, he'd accomplished what few men had—turned a business into a Fortune 500 company.

He'd never disappointed his grandfather in the past and had no intention of doing so now. Besides, should he have refused to embark on this ridiculous quest, his grandfather had promised to dethrone him and scratch his name off the will.

The will issue didn't bother Nelson as much as the thought of losing power. He was at his best as commander and chief—or so he believed. But his grandfather had charged him with refusing to listen to his employees' ideas and not allowing others to lead—in essence, he'd accused Nelson of being a poor leader.

The argument that he hadn't listened to others because they'd yet to supply better ideas than his own had not gone over well with the old man. In the end,

Nelson had conceded that taking orders from someone else for three months wouldn't be too painful. But damn it, his grandfather could have chosen a different job to prove his point. Nelson knew zip about farming.

Albeit grudgingly, Nelson applauded the old man's cunningness. His grandfather had stuck him in a job that he'd had no experience with, forcing him to rely on someone else's guidance. He'd received little information about the widow, what crops she grew or even how many acres her farm encompassed.

On the bright side, the widow was probably a great cook. He hadn't had three square meals a day in years. And the fresh air and sunshine would do him good. Besides, it wasn't as if he couldn't keep tabs on the office while away. When the widow went to bed, he intended to use his BlackBerry to check in with his staff and answer e-mails.

After fifteen minutes of nothing but wooded brush alongside the road, green pastures appeared. He slowed the car and searched for the dead tree. Gnarled limbs bleached gray with time sprang into view sooner than he expected. Since he'd been the only vehicle on the road the past half hour, he eased his foot off the gas and the Jaguar slowed to thirty miles an hour. He followed the curve and a moment later a sign announced Four Corners 5 miles.

Now that he'd almost arrived at his destination, Nelson's gut clenched. He wasn't nervous about the physical labor involved in farming. Wasn't even worried that he understood nothing about the agricultural business. His apprehension stemmed from his fear of being away from the office for an extended period of time. Unlike others, Nelson did not work to live. He lived to work.

On occasion, he wondered if the constant need to keep busy was an inherited genetic disorder. Neither of his brothers harbored a compulsion to toil away 24-7. Why him? Even on those rare occasions when he wanted nothing more than to return home, put his feet up on the coffee table and watch a football game, more often than not he opened his briefcase and became sidetracked. By the time his eyes grew tired from reading, the game had ended and he'd missed every play.

His foot firmly on the gas pedal once again, Nelson zipped by some businesses at the intersection of RR 7 and Mueller Road, then another sign: Thank You For Visiting Four Corners.

What the heck? He slammed his foot on the brake for the second time in less than an hour. Shifting into Reverse, he returned to the intersection he'd blown through. He pulled on to the shoulder and studied the four brick-and-stone-fronted buildings—each occupying a corner.

The words *quaint* and *artsy* entered his mind as he took in the hanging flower baskets outside Flo's Diner. Ethel's Diner sat catty-corner to Flo's. A couple of rocking chairs and an old claw-foot tub overflowing with plants decorated her business.

The Fuel Stop and Fred's Pack 'n' Save claimed the other two corners. Fred's business had colorful writing across the glass windows, advertising in-store specials, and a garbage can chained to the light pole outside.

Four businesses…four corners…nothing else. No movie theater. No pizza parlor. Not even a bar.

Movement near the front window of Flo's Diner caught his attention. A waitress with blond pigtails moved about, wiping off tables—probably a local. He'd ask inside about the Tanner farm. If no one had heard of the place, he'd return to Chicago and end this wild-goose chase his grandfather had sent him on.

"OH…MY…LORD. Would you look at that." Flo smacked her bubble gum and pointed to the front window.

"Don't tell me Billy Joe finally bought the Mustang he's been jawing about for the past year and a half." Ellen Tanner didn't bother glancing toward her boss's long neon-pink fingernail. She equated Billy Joe to a big black fly—pesky, always buzzing around her and someone she just flat-out wanted to slap at with a wet dishtowel.

"No Mustang. Can't say for sure what kind of car. Fancy, though. Must have cost a pretty penny."

Interest piqued; Ellen peered out the window. "Oh, my," she murmured, unaware the sugar shaker she'd been filling overflowed on to the blue Formica tabletop. "He's lost." Had to be. No man that handsome had ever stopped in Four Corners on purpose.

"You think?" Flo popped a bubble. "Yeah, probably." She left the lunch counter and zigzagged through the tables to pause at Ellen's side. "I can't remember the last time I saw a man in dress pants. You?"

"Nope." Ellen craned her neck to gain a better view of the newcomer as he made his way to the door. The men around these parts wore jeans or overalls, even to church. Only for a funeral or wedding did a man drag a suit out of the closet.

"He's headin' in here." Flo scurried across the room, patting her graying bob in place. "How's my hair?" she asked.

The older woman had great bone structure and appeared ten years younger than her true age—early fifties. "Your hair's fine," Ellen assured her.

"Hey, Flo," the lone customer in the diner called. "How about a refill on my coffee?"

"Get your own refill, Howard. Can't you see I'm busy?" Smile pasted on her face, Flo stood ready to pounce. When the door opened, she gushed, "Welcome to Flo's Diner. I'm Flo." She pumped the man's hand like a tire jack.

"Good afternoon," he answered, his rich baritone voice eliciting a silent sigh from Ellen.

Handsome, deep voice and at least a couple of inches over six feet—the total package demanded respect. Ellen had no idea what he did for a living, but she'd bet every dollar in her Folgers-coffee-can bank he wasn't a salesman.

Flo motioned him to the lunch counter. "Stopping for a bite to eat or just coffee?"

"I'll take a club sandwich if you've got one." Without a glance at Ellen, he sat on a stool two seats from Howard, who still held out his coffee cup for a refill.

It figured the stranger wouldn't notice her. The only man who ever paid Ellen any mind was Billy Joe—because he wanted her farm. They'd gone through school in the same grade, but he'd run with a wild crowd and Ellen had been Miss Goody Two-shoes—until she'd ended up pregnant the summer before she'd entered twelfth grade. After her husband, Buck, had died in a construction accident a little over a year ago, Billy Joe had become a nuisance—a big, painful oozing canker in her backside.

Ignoring the stranger, she considered the mess she'd made with the sugar shaker. *You seriously need to get a life, Ellen.*

"Coffee, soda, water?" Flo's voice carried across the tables.

"Water will be fine."

Probably a health nut. Ellen searched for the plastic bin she used to clear the dirty dishes from the tables and spotted it at the end of the lunch counter. Shrugging, she bent at the waist and swept the spilled sugar into the pocket of her apron, then brushed the remaining grains onto the floor.

"Passing through or staying a spell in Four Corners?" Flo asked.

"Here on business."

Go, Flo, go. Give the older woman ten minutes and she'd have the man's life story. Not that Ellen blamed her boss. Like herself, Flo had been born and raised in Four Corners. Flo's deceased parents had left the diner to her. Twenty years ago, she'd sold the property and run off with an insurance man from West Virginia. After two years she'd returned to town a disillusioned and divorced woman. She'd bought the business back, and had lived in Four Corners—single and bored to death—ever since.

Ellen envied her boss. For a short time Flo had had the opportunity to experience something other than cornfields and cows. As a little girl—truthfully, up until she'd gotten pregnant—Ellen had dreamed of leaving the farm and moving to the city. She studied the fancy black car parked outside—a bold reminder that life didn't always accommodate a person's dreams.

Flo skipped into the kitchen and two minutes later returned with the stranger's order. Howard continued to wave his cup in the air, until Flo finally thunked the coffeepot on the counter in front of him. She shuffled back to the other man. "You a feed salesman?"

Cheeks bulging with lunch meat, he frowned. Guess the guy wasn't a feed salesman.

"Fancy wheels you got out there. You a gambler?" Flo could be such a pest.

"I don't gamble."

Pink fingernails drummed against the countertop. "A movie star?"

That brought a grin to his face.

Ellen edged a bit closer to better scrutinize the man's profile. He wasn't drop-dead-gorgeous—more like the boy next door, but with rough edges. He had a large nose and an intriguing scar along one side of his square jaw. His mocha-colored hair was mussed—

not his preferred style, she suspected. She wasn't sure about the color of his eyes, but figured they were the same dark brown as his eyebrows. Appealing. Sexy.

Out of your league.

"What about sports? You play hockey or baseball?" Flo refused to give up.

"I crewed at Harvard."

Harvard? Yeah, he had the look of an Ivy Leaguer.

Flo set a slice of key lime pie in front of Mr. Harvard. "Never heard of crewing."

"Rowing. Four-man boat. I was the bow man. Sat in the back and coached my teammates."

"Well, the only thing we use a boat for around these parts is to catch fish. You gonna tell me what business you have in Four Corners?"

"I'm searching for the Tanner farm."

Ellen's hand froze in midair as she reached for the dirty ketchup bottle on the table.

"What business do you have with the Tanners?"

Her heart pounding, Ellen's mind raced. Was the man a creditor? She'd mailed a payment to the credit-card company last week, but the check had only covered the finance charge on the credit card. Or maybe he was a county tax assessor intending to inform her that they'd refused her request for an extension. The man claimed he wasn't a salesman, so she doubted he planned to sell her a cemetery plot. Had her deceased husband been involved in something illegal like gambling? Deep in thought, she almost missed the stranger's answer.

"I need to speak with Ellen Tanner. Patrick Mc-

Kade corresponded with her several weeks ago and arranged for a hired hand to help on her farm this summer."

"Oh, yeah. Ellen mentioned that a while back."

"I understand Mrs. Tanner is a widow."

Flo nodded. "Been just over a year since Buck died. She has a boy named Seth."

"How old is her son?"

"Thirteen as of this past Christmas."

"I assume he helps his mother with the farm."

Flo shrugged. "Seth's a typical boy. Would rather hang out with his friends than do chores."

"The boy shouldn't be allowed to shirk his responsibilities."

Ellen's ire rose. She acknowledged she was having trouble with Seth since Buck had passed away. And yes, her son *should* be helping out more. But darn it, who'd asked the guy for his opinion?

"How old is Mrs. Tanner?" Five large bites of pie disappeared in record time. The know-it-all had a sweet tooth.

"Why don't you ask her yourself?" Flo motioned across the room. "She's right there."

The handsome stranger swiveled on the stool. Stared. Then snorted. "A teenager? If she's a farmer, I'll eat my shoe."

Insulted, embarrassed and a tad amused, Ellen wandered closer to the counter. She toed off her sneaker, flipped it into the air, caught it with one hand, then slapped the shoe on the counter. "How about eating mine, instead?"

Chapter Two

Nelson glanced at the size 6 stamped on the inside of the white canvas shoe, then at the woman whose foot it had enclosed. Blond pigtails, a fresh-from-the-farm face—smattering of freckles across the nose, soft blue eyes framed by light-brown lashes, a pair of dainty eyebrows and a mouth that should have been too wide for the heart-shaped face. Sweet and innocent. *"You're* Ellen Tanner?"

The dainty chin jutted. "And who are you?"

Cross off *sweet* and make that *sarcastic.* "Nelson McKade."

Her eyes rounded into big blue circles. "Patrick McKade's grandson?"

No mistaking the disbelief in her voice. "Yes, I'm his grandson, and you don't look like a farmer."

The blue circles narrowed to slits. "And you're no farmhand."

All that belligerence made his pulse race and his heart thump erratically. Never had a woman had such an effect on him. "I'm the CEO of McKade Import-Export. I run the Chicago office."

In a battle of wills, they glared at each other, neither willing to break eye contact. The miniature bully's blue slits narrowed even further, until he wondered if she could see anything.

"I've been conned." Her bare foot slapped the linoleum floor.

"No, I've been conned." What did Ms. Daisy Maisy care if her summer hand was a greenhorn? Nelson had no experience driving a tractor or harvesting a crop, but he'd approach his responsibilities the same way he tackled a day at the office—work until he'd accomplished every task.

The bell on the door clanged. Nelson had forgotten about the other customer at the lunch counter. The older man had left without a word and now headed across the street to Ethel's Diner. Wouldn't be long before news spread that the widow Tanner's farm hand had arrived in town.

Flo, who'd been quiet until now, mumbled something about checking pies in the oven, then vanished into the kitchen, leaving him and Farmer Blonde alone. Nelson seized advantage of Ellen's distraction. The pink T-shirt she wore had a picture of Tweety Bird on the front. The overalls did nothing to enhance her figure, which appeared trim and fit beneath the ten yards of denim. And the dainty toes on her shoeless bare foot sported peach-colored nails decorated with tiny white flowers. Amused by the sight, he grinned.

"What's so funny?"

"The women in my office wouldn't be caught dead with flowers painted on their toenails."

"You figure out a better way to spend a Saturday night around here and I'll consider it."

Great. If the hard work didn't kill him, boredom would.

Ellen rubbed her temple, no doubt suffering the same malady as Nelson—a full-blown migraine. "Your grandfather insisted you wanted to take a sabbatical from your job."

"Not exactly."

"I'm all ears." Five toes tapped agitatedly against the floor, creating the illusion of flowers blowing in the wind.

Impatient little thing. "I'm here because I have to be."

"And you have to be…because?"

Never one to shy from the truth, he confessed, "My grandfather believed I should be taught a lesson."

The corners of her mouth curved upward, lending a decidedly sexy charm to the pixie face. "Couldn't he have just spanked you?"

Mesmerized by her mouth, Nelson didn't immediately react to the comment. Then her sarcasm registered and he grinned. "If given the choice, I would have picked the spanking. But grandfather insists I learn my lesson on your farm."

Dainty eyebrows scrunched over her nose. "What lesson is that?"

"Acquiescence."

The flower toes ceased moving. "Acquiescence?"

"I don't receive orders very well," he conceded.

"How are you going to work for me if you won't do what I tell you to?"

"I promise to be on my best behavior. Three months max and I'm back in my office and out of your hair." Speaking of hair…he had the insane urge to yank her pigtail. Were the shiny strands as silky as they seemed?

"Your grandfather said you had experience in shipping. I'd assumed you were employed as a dock worker." Her gaze raked over his body. "You don't have the body of a man who unloads freight all day."

This was a first—coming up short in a woman's eyes. The idea that the widow found him lacking nipped his ego like a nasty dog bite. "No, I don't juggle freight for a living, but I intend to give you an honest day's labor."

Blue eyes deepened to indigo as she mulled over his promise. "Farmers don't keep executive hours."

Little imp. "I'm at the office by five in the morning and don't arrive home until eight or nine at night."

"We're up at four-thirty and in bed by nine."

What was this—a game of tit for tat? "I can handle the hours."

"I don't cook three meals a day."

So much for the room and board advertised with the low wages.

She nibbled her lip again. A nervous habit? Or something she did when she wasn't being truthful?

"I'll eat here once in a while." The club sandwich had tasted fine. By Labor Day he'd probably have sampled every item on the menu. "And there's always the diner across the road."

"Ethel can't cook worth spit!" Flo shouted from the kitchen.

Ellen smiled, the gesture chasing the worry from her pretty blue eyes.

"You mind telling me why you're working as a waitress when you have a farm to run?" The smile slid off her face, dragging the sparkle in her eyes along with it. He should have kept his mouth shut.

"I doubt you'd be interested in the whys. Suffice it to say, I wait tables to make ends meet. You'd be amazed at the food a thirteen-year-old boy puts away in one day."

Nelson recalled how he and his brothers had astonished their grandfather's cook by the amount of food they'd consumed during adolescence. Didn't farmers grow most of their food?

"We have a small vegetable garden." Reading minds must be an inherent trait in rural people.

"According to my son, tomatoes don't stand a chance against a Quarter Pounder from McDonald's."

Although fast food didn't excite him, he sympathized with the boy. He'd rather throw tomatoes than eat them. "What does your son do while you're working?"

"I have weekends off and my shift ends at three, so I'm able to beat the school bus to the farm."

He checked his Rolex. "It's four o'clock."

"The band is having an end-of-the-year party today."

"What instrument does your son play?"

"The trombone. Your grandfather mentioned in his letter that you wanted to marry and have kids of your own soon."

Nice segue. "Grandfather lied." Just because his

younger brother, Aaron, had ended up engaged to *his* boss after learning his life lesson on a construction crew didn't mean Nelson planned the same with this woman. "And where teenagers are concerned I don't have a clue."

"Welcome to my world."

"But you're a mother. Shouldn't you—"

"I gave birth to a human being. I'm not sure what my son is right now…possibly an alien."

"He's a difficult kid, then?"

"No more than any other boy his age." She focused on the front window. "He's had a difficult time since his daddy's death last year."

Nelson wondered if Ellen still struggled with the loss of her husband. "Your son isn't going to be a problem for me, is he?"

"You won't have to worry about Seth."

"I won't?"

"Nope. Because you won't be working on my farm." Ellen Tanner grabbed her sneaker off the counter, wiggled her foot into it, then stuffed her hand into the front pocket of her apron and pulled out a handful of change—sugar-coated nickels, dimes, pennies and quarters. She slapped the coins on the counter, sending white particles spewing in all directions. "That's all I have to compensate you for your time and trouble. Good day." Chin in the air, she disappeared into the kitchen.

"Wait just a damn minute," Nelson called.

"Tell him I left through the back door," Ellen whispered to Flo, who stood at the sink, arms in suds up to her elbows, mouth sagging.

Ellen slipped behind the door and hid from sight. No way was that teen-ignorant man residing on her farm. Seth had his faults, but she loved him dearly and refused to sentence him to a summer hanging around a grown man in a big pout.

She sensed Nelson McKade was bull-headed and considered himself right and everyone else wrong. Besides, having a city slicker—a constant reminder of the life she'd always dreamed of—shoved under her nose for weeks on end was enough to give her the shakes.

"Where is she?" The question met Ellen's ears seconds before the door met her nose.

"Yeow!"

A masculine hand grabbed the edge of the door, then a handsome face wavered in front of her watering eyes. "My God, are you all right? Where did the door hit you?"

Before she could answer, callused hands cupped her jaw. "Your nose is bleeding." He plugged her nostril with his big thumb, wrapped an arm around her shoulder and guided her to a folding chair next to the sink. "Get some ice, Flo." He knelt on one knee, thumb still shoved up her nose, and smoothed a hand down her pigtail.

She would never have guessed Nelson McKade had a gentle side to him. A side she wouldn't mind exploring if things were different. If she were different.

"I'm sorry, Ellen." He set his hand on her thigh to balance himself, and the warmth of his long fingers seeped through the denim material and right into her skin. She shivered at the tingly sensation.

"Are you cold?" He didn't wait for an answer. Not that she expected him to. The man had a talent for asking and answering his own questions. "Flo, bring a blanket or something. Ellen's going into shock."

Oh, for God's sake. Her entire face might be numb, but she wasn't about to pass out.

"I know it hurts. The ice should help the pain." He caressed her cheek, his breath fanning her mouth, making her forget the pain. Making her imagine what his kiss would taste like.

How long had it been since a man had laid hands on her? Patted her hair? Her cheek? Stuck his thumb in her nose?

Flo returned from the storage room and draped a sweater across Ellen's shoulders, then handed Nelson a towel filled with ice cubes. He let go of her thigh and carefully held the towel to the bridge of her nose.

"Maybe you should see a doctor," Flo suggested.

"My nose is fine," Ellen insisted, sounding like an idiot, with one nostril plugged. She swung her head sideways and Nelson's thumb popped out. Gesturing to the blood, she advised, "Wash your hand."

He wiped his thumb on the paper towel Flo had fetched, then pressed his fingertips against her forehead, her cheekbones, her jaw. "Nothing feels broken, but you're beginning to bruise." His finger rubbed the skin beneath her eye.

"You better drive her out to the farm. She's probably concussed." Flo's eyes twinkled.

"No one's driving me anywhere." She swatted at the ice pack. "Let me up. The cows need to be milked."

"I'll follow in my car." Nelson stood, then offered a hand.

Intuition warned she could argue with Nelson Mc-Kade until her whole face became black and blue, and he still wouldn't back down. Fine. Let him follow her. One look-see at the farm and he'd tuck tail and run. "Suit yourself." Ignoring his outstretched hand, she marched from the kitchen.

Cows?

Wishing the steering wheel were his grandfather's neck, Nelson squeezed until his knuckles threatened to pop out of joint. Would there never be an end to the old man's surprises? First, Nelson had expected Ellen Tanner to be an elderly widow, *not* a pretty young widow. Second, he assumed he'd be harvesting corn or alfalfa, *not* milking dairy cows.

As he followed the rattletrap truck through the entrance gate, he noticed that the wooden sign, Tanner Farm, hung crookedly from the corner fence post. "Whoa!" He swerved, avoiding a huge pothole in the drive. A moment later, he swung the wheel in the opposite direction to evade another crater. He should be driving a 69-ton Abrams tank to navigate this maze of landmines. He guessed at least five years had passed since a fresh layer of gravel had been laid down on the driveway.

Ellen parked next to the barn, left the truck and disappeared inside the structure. Nelson stopped the car, now covered in a coating of gray dust, by the front porch. He shut off the motor and stared out the wind-

shield. Some quintessential farmhouse—an architec-
turally boring one-story white box. Where were the
shutters, the wraparound porch with rocking chairs
facing west and the hound dog lounging in the sun?
There wasn't even a welcome mat on the cement
stoop. Except for the healthy hundred-year-old oak
tree shading the yard, the place had a depressing feel.

A quick scan of the barnyard netted no chickens
pecking the ground. No pigs rolling in the mud. Still
no dog. Didn't every farm have at least one dog and
several cats wandering around? There was nothing
homey or warm about the residence, as though the
people living here would rather be someplace else.

A flash of pink caught his attention. Ellen left the
smaller, graying white barn through a side door,
crossed under a covered walkway, then entered a larger, rectangular, green steel barn. He noticed the structure had two-foot vents running along its steeply
pitched roof. A moment later she reappeared in coveralls, leading a cow into the white barn. For several
minutes he watched her repeat the process, until she'd
retrieved eight cows.

Obviously, she planned to ignore him. Might as
well put an end to her wishful thinking. He left the car
and pocketed his keys. Halfway to the barn, he cursed.
A brown glob oozed from the sides of his shoe. Cow
poop. He should have stopped at the Farm and Fleet
he'd passed earlier in the afternoon and purchased a
pair of sturdy boots.

Dragging his heel against the ground, he continued
to the barn. He paused inside the door, allowing his

eyes to adjust to the dim interior. The scent of disinfectant greeted his nostrils first, followed by an earthy mixture of animal and hay.

In the middle of the barn, Ellen rubbed a big, black, wet nose and murmured nonsensical words. Between every two animals sat a trolley containing two stainless-steel canisters with four rubber suction hoses attached to the cow's teats. The quiet slurp of the mini milking machines hummed in the air.

Fanny Farmer moved up and down the aisle, cooing to her charges. Petting their heads. Like good little kids, the cows remained quiet during the milking process. He had to smile at Ellen's attire—a jumpsuit that resembled something an auto mechanic would wear to protect his clothes. She'd stuffed her pigtails under a blue paper cap and clean black rubber boots covered her feet. "What's up with the outfit?" he called out.

The cows immediately mooed and shifted in the stalls. Pressing a finger to her mouth, Ellen commanded, "Keep your voice down."

"Why?" he whispered.

"Nervous cows don't give milk," she explained as she moved toward him.

He stepped in her direction, but froze when she held up a hand.

"Stop right there. You can't enter the milking barn dressed like that."

"I have to put on that getup?" He nodded to her outfit.

"Yes. The barn should be kept as germfree as possible."

"All right. Where do I find another jumpsuit?"

Her mouth dropped open.

Had she hoped that after he'd seen the cows and sniffed the air in the barn he'd scurry back to Chicago? Boy, was she in for a big surprise. "Consider this, Ellen Tanner. Whether you choose to pay me or not, I'm here for the summer. It's your call. I lounge around your house and do nothing, or you teach me to milk cows."

"I think there's something you should know," she hedged.

"What?"

"I lied to your grandfather."

"You're not a widow?" He glanced over his shoulder, expecting a hulking giant to jump out of a dark corner and threaten him with a pitchfork.

"No. I mean, yes, I'm a widow." Her gaze attached itself to the barn door. "I fibbed when I told your grandfather I needed a man to do chores."

"If you don't require the help, then what do you want a man for?" Her attention shifted from the door to his body. A flash of heat raced through Nelson. *No way!* She'd hired him to…to…have sex with her?

She must have read his thoughts, because she snarled, "I need someone to keep tabs on my son."

The sting of disappointment surprised him. "You desire a babysitter?" *But not me?*

"Not a babysitter. A companion."

"Lady, I'm thirty-seven years old. I don't hang out with teenagers."

"Suit yourself." There went the chin in the air

again. "If you won't keep track of Seth, then you can just drive that fancy car of yours back to Chicago."

The woman was serious. For the first time in a long time, Nelson wasn't sure how to proceed. He'd faced some heated moments in the boardroom over the years, but nothing compared with the fire spitting from the two big blue eyes five feet away.

The longer he studied Ellen, the more he saw through her false bravado. His chest tightened with compassion. The woman single-handedly ran a dairy farm, worked a second job and was raising a son alone. His employees didn't toil that hard and he paid them a hell of a lot of money. "I'll supervise your boy on one condition." Oh, hell. His grandfather insisted he learn how to take orders, not boss the boss.

"Condition?" A cute crinkle formed between her eyebrows and he resisted the temptation to smooth it away with his finger.

"You allow me to help with the cows."

"But—"

"If your son is anything like I was at thirteen, he'll sleep for twelve hours a day. I might as well be useful until he wakes up."

Expecting her to balk at his demand, she surprised him by ending their sparring match. "Fine."

He should be grateful she hadn't put up a fuss, but in truth he found her stubbornness a challenge and had anticipated going another round with her. "Where do I find a pair—"

"In there." She nodded to the doorway on Nelson's right. "Scrub your hands with the antibacterial soap.

Don't forget a cap. And—" she frowned at his feet "—never, ever, walk through the milking barn with poopy shoes. Buck's old boots are under the sink. Wear those."

Five minutes later, Nelson emerged from the wash-room feeling like a…a…

"Who's the dweeb, Mom?"

Dweeb? Nelson admitted he probably did look like a doofus in blue coveralls and a fast-food hair net. If his brothers could see him now, they'd split their guts laughing.

Wearing a the-world-sucks glare on his face, Nelson's new charge lounged in the barn doorway with a backpack slung over one shoulder.

"Seth, be polite." Ellen's reprimand sounded muf-fled. Probably due to the fact she was lifting one of the large stainless-steel milk cans from the trolley.

Forgetting about the kid, Nelson rushed over to help. As he relieved her of the heavy burden, he noticed a purple bruise forming beneath her right eye and felt like a schmuck for having smacked her face with the door.

"This is Mr. McKade. I've hired him to help out this summer." She didn't have to act so resigned. "Mr. McKade, this is my son, Seth Tanner."

"Hello, Seth. Pleasure to meet you." He couldn't very well shake the teen's hand until he dumped the milk somewhere. "Where does this go?"

"Over here." She led the way to the rear of the barn, where four large canisters lined the wall. "These are the collecting cans. When the can is full, we insert an in-can turbine cooler to bring the temperature of the milk down."

Now that Nelson thought about it, the container in his hand felt warm. "What's the temperature of the milk when it leaves the cow?"

"Around 101 degrees. The turbine coolers lower the temperature to forty degrees and keep it there until the milk truck arrives. The truck picks up every two days or so."

Careful not to spill a drop, Nelson poured the milk into the canister. "Any of the others ready to be emptied?"

"Not yet."

"What should I do now?"

"Nothing. Wait here." Ellen went to her son, leaving Nelson to twiddle his thumbs. Deciding he should become better acquainted with the cows, he wandered over to the one named Betty and patted her rump.

"How did the band party go?" Nelson overheard Ellen ask the boy.

"Okay, I guess." The teen sneered at Nelson. "He don't act like no farm hand."

Smart kid.

Ignoring the rude comment, Ellen asked, "What finals do you have tomorrow?" She lifted a hand to ruffle her son's hair, but the boy moved his head away.

"English and art."

"Get a snack in the house, then go hit the books."

"I'll study later. Brad got a new video game. His mom said I could—"

"School first, Seth. There'll be plenty of time to play video games this summer."

As soon as the grumbling teen exited the barn, Ellen hissed, "Step back."

Ignorant of what barn rule he'd broken now, Nelson shifted away from the cow's rear end.

Cheeks flushed with fury, she warned, "Don't ever stand behind a cow. Cows see everything around them except what's immediately in back of their hindquarters."

"Aren't dairy cows tame like house pets?"

"The cows know me, my voice and my touch. You're a stranger to them." She rubbed her forehead. "This isn't going to work."

No way was he giving her a reason to boot him off the farm. "If I have to make friends with them before they trust me, then I'll do it. Tell me how."

After a long pause, she instructed, "Keep your voice low and calm. Approach the animal from the front and use slow hand movements when you touch them."

"That's it?"

"And don't stand to the side of the cow, either. When they get nervous, they lash out to the front and the side. The last thing I wish for this summer is a call to 911 because you got yourself kicked in the head."

A hoof to the head was exactly what he deserved for agreeing to appease his grandfather. He signaled to the animals in the stalls. "So this is what you want me to do every day?"

"No. You'll wash the equipment and haul the milk

to the holding cans. I'll clean the cows' udders and hook them up to the suction tubes."

"Why do you get to have all the fun?"

"Try doing it for twenty years and then tell me if you still think it's fun." She walked down the aisle, detaching the suction tubes from the udders. When all the cows had been unhooked, she pushed a button on an electrical panel in the wall and the stall doors opened automatically. Like trained circus performers, the animals moved forward and exited the barn into a grazing pasture.

"How many cows do you have?" he asked.

"Right now, twenty-four."

"How often do you milk them?"

"Twice a day."

He added up the time she'd spent on the first eight cows, subtracted fifteen minutes for interruptions, and figured the milking took Ellen at least a few hours to do by herself. She spent six hours out of each day in this barn. And that didn't include cleaning the equipment, the barns or feeding the cows. Then she waited tables for five or six hours and somehow managed to take care of her son's needs. Crazy lady. It was only a matter of time before she collapsed from total exhaustion or suffered a nervous breakdown. "Should I get the next group of cows?"

"No. But I'd appreciate you checking on Seth." Her challenging stare stopped the protest in the middle of his throat.

"All right. I'll see if he's studying, then return to help clean up."

"Don't bother. There's not enough time today to show you how to wash the equipment."

His first instinct was to challenge her, but then his grandfather's face popped into his mind and he snapped his mouth shut. He'd show the old man he could follow an order. "Fine. Where do you want me to put my things?"

"Things?"

"Clothes. Toiletries."

She glanced over her shoulder. "I fixed up a room for you in the other barn."

No. "You're making me sleep with the cows?"

"I'm sure you'll get along just fine with your new roommates."

Chapter Three

Acquiescence. Acquiescence. Acquiescence.

Nelson wondered whether there were any how-to books on self-hypnosis. If repeating the word in his mind didn't brainwash him, the process would at least calm his growing irritation with Fanny Farmer aka Ellen Tanner. In a controlled voice, he insisted, "You honestly expect me to sleep in a barn."

An unladylike snort rewarded his calm demeanor. "Sorry, but the local Hilton is booked for the summer."

"I assumed the room-and-board offer in your Help Wanted ad included decent accommodations. Isn't there an extra bedroom in the house?"

"You can't sleep in the house with Seth and me. What would people think?"

"I wouldn't be *sleeping* with you or Seth." He shuddered when he imagined her waspish tongue in bed. On the other hand, the notion of kissing her unruly mouth into submission intrigued him.

"Typical big-city mentality." She planted her fists

on her hips and glared. "I have to set an example for my son."

He admired her for that, but—

"And I don't want to give him another reason to be at odds with me."

At odds with her? "He's thirteen and he lives on a farm. He knows about sex, Ellen. I'll make sure he understands that we aren't having it."

Her face paled, causing the freckles across the bridge of her nose to pop out like leopard spots. "This isn't going to—"

"I'll sleep in the barn," he blurted, the concession souring his stomach.

Her fists slid off her hips and her shoulders slumped in defeat.

Maybe he wasn't what she'd hoped for in a hired hand, but he deserved a chance.

Why should you warrant a second chance when you've never give your employees the same opportunity? "Shut up," he mumbled to the voice in his head.

"Pardon me?"

"I asked where the room was."

Her dark expression warned him to expect another tongue-lashing, but she simply grumbled, "The small storage compartment at the end of the big barn."

"*Big* meaning the green steel structure?"

She nodded.

"The one where all the cows hang out, waiting to be milked?"

Another nod.

"The one that stinks like manure?"

Her head bobbed again; only, this time she retreated a step.

"Where am I supposed to shower?"

"I suppose you can use the bathroom in the house." The reluctant acceptance of the situation resonated loud and clear in her voice.

He clenched his jaw until he thought the bone might splinter. He should consider himself fortunate he didn't have to use a hose to bathe. "I can't change your mind about helping you right now?"

There went the chin…up in the air again.

A battled waged inside him. He didn't feel right about a woman, albeit a strong willed and capable one, doing this kind of work alone, even if it did give him more practice following commands. "Fine," he muttered, the word almost choking him. He spun away, but her hand on his arm stopped him.

"Please don't tell Seth I hired you to keep track of him."

The immature urge to refuse her request rankled. Used to dealing with hardheaded businessmen on a daily basis, Nelson felt baffled by this woman's ability to provoke. *Have you considered that she sets you on edge because you're attracted to her?* "No."

"What?" Her blue eyes rounded.

"I mean, no, I won't tell Seth."

"Thank you." Without another word, she pivoted on her rubber-booted heel and marched off to retrieve the next group of beloved bovines.

Nelson contemplated phoning his grandfather to explain the situation, and then begging for a change of venue for his life lesson. But he knew better than to complain to the old man. Besides, he himself hated whiners.

He returned to the washroom and removed the coveralls, cap and boots. On the way to the house, he retrieved his BlackBerry from his car. The urge to phone his younger brother, Aaron, pissed him off. Nelson had always been the one in charge. The solid, steady guy in the family. The man everyone looked up to. Why all of a sudden did he wish for reassurance from his baby brother?

Oh, hell. He leaned against the front fender, where he had a clean view of Ellen coaxing the cows into the milking barn, and dialed Aaron's cell number.

"Nelson?"

"Yeah, it's me."

"What's up?"

Already regretting the call, he grappled for words. "I hit the wrong—"

Laughter burst through the connection. "How's the life lesson going?"

"Not funny, Aaron. Our grandfather needs a psychological evaluation."

"Pop won't say where you are, but if you spill the beans, I'll drop in for a visit this summer." The wicked glee in his brother's voice tempted Nelson to reveal his location.

"I know how you worry. Rest assured, Ryan and I are keeping tabs on the Chicago office."

Aaron taking care of things? He cringed. His brother would rather offer the employees a week's paid vacation and shut the doors until Nelson returned.

Give the guy credit. Aaron's doing something right if his community-enhancement program in L.A. is garnering positive press for McKade Import-Export. "How's Jennifer?"

"She's great. But we're moving up the wedding."

The last time he'd heard, Aaron and Jennifer had planned their nuptials for around Christmas. "Why?"

"Promise you won't tell Pop or Ryan?"

He wouldn't promise anything. "What kind of trouble did you get into now, Aaron?"

"A good kind. Jennifer's pregnant."

"Pregnant?" His baby brother was going to be a father? How could this have happened? Nelson felt very old and very much alone at hearing Aaron's pronouncement. "When you mess up, you mess up big."

Silence greeted the comment. "We didn't *mess up*, Nelson," Ryan insisted in a steely tone. "Jennifer and I planned to start a family right away. It happened a little sooner than we expected is all."

Regretting his harsh comment, Nelson swallowed hard and said, "Congratulations, little brother. When's the baby due?"

"Late January or early February. We're hoping to book a Saturday wedding in August at her church in Santa Angelita. Will Pop be okay with marrying in Los Angeles?"

"Pop will be thrilled to be a great-grandfather. He won't care where the ceremony is as long as you get married."

"Don't spill the beans. I want to be the first to tell them."

"Promise." Nelson decided to end the conversation. His brother's news had unsettled him. "I need to go."

"Not so fast. Pop said he found you a job in the agricultural business. What are you—"

"You're breaking up, Aaron. I can't hear…" Nelson disconnected the call, ignoring the guilty sting at his rudeness.

A snort sounded from somewhere behind him. Startled, Nelson glanced at the front door, where Ellen's son eyed him through the screen. "Fancy cell phone. That a rich man's toy?"

"It's called a BlackBerry. Ever heard of those?"

The kid came outside, letting the door bang shut. "Ah, let me think…" He tapped a finger against his temple. "Yeah, man, I've got two in my backpack."

Just what he dreamed of—a summer with an overgrown brat. Reining in his temper, Nelson insisted, "Go ahead." He held out the device, amused by the way the boy slowly, very slowly, descended the steps. The kid acted as if he couldn't care less, but the excitement in Seth's eyes told Nelson otherwise.

"What else does it do?" Seth ditched the tough-guy attitude for the moment.

"E-mail. Calendar. Planner and phone. A couple of games." After a few moments of silence, Nelson inquired, "Are you in any computer courses in school?"

"Yeah. But the computer lab sucks."

"Do you have a computer in the house?"

The gnarly expression returned. "My mom ain't

exactly raking in the dough milking cows." He gestured around him. "In case you ain't—"

"Haven't," Nelson corrected the boy.

"Haven't what?"

"It's not *ain't*. It's *haven't*."

Smirking, Seth continued, "In case you *haven't* noticed, we ain't rich."

Nelson had noticed. Noticed that it had been years since the white barn had received a fresh coat of paint. Noticed that the gutters were practically falling off the house. Noticed that Ellen's truck was on its last legs. How could he *not* notice that the boy's deceased father had left Ellen and the farm in poor shape?

He'd have plenty of time to kill supervising Seth. It wouldn't hurt for him to evaluate Ellen's assets. He was positive he could figure out a way to improve her overall fiscal situation. Shoot, running a farm wasn't much different from managing import-export accounts. "Any chance your school will get new computers soon?"

"Nope. We gotta use 'em till they blow up." He handed over the BlackBerry. "How come you ain't helping my mom?"

Remembering his promise not to mention babysitting duties, Nelson asked, "How come *you're* not helping your mother?"

Shoulders stiff, Seth insisted, "I'm studying for finals."

Hoping to avoid an argument, Nelson asked, "Want any help?"

Another snort—a trait Seth must have inherited from his mother. "Like *you* could help me."

The kid needed a lesson in manners. Had Nelson treated his grandfather with such disrespect, he'd have had a bar of soap stuffed into his mouth. "What subject?"

"English."

Nelson hated high-school English. He preferred math. Numbers never changed and they couldn't be misinterpreted. "Maybe I can help."

"What do you know about *Romeo and Juliet?*"

Only that Romeo should have looked elsewhere for love. "I had to read the play in school."

"It's so lame."

"No argument there."

The boy eyed him suspiciously, not sure whether to believe Nelson. "I have to write two pages on the stupid theme of love."

Love—a topic Nelson had little experience with. The man-woman kind, anyway. He'd had two serious relationships during his thirty-seven years and both had ended badly. He doubted there was a woman on earth who would understand his drive to succeed and willingly accept a backseat to his career. For the past two years he'd dated sporadically but had never allowed the relationship to turn serious. "I believe I can help."

"No shi—" The boy caught Nelson's scowl and swallowed the rest of the swear word.

"Lead the way." He followed the kid inside, wondering which was the lesser of two evils—milking cows with a wasp-tongued woman or explaining love to a teenage boy.

TIRED, CRANKY and disgusted by her eagerness to hurry to the house and the man waiting there, Ellen purposefully slowed her steps as she left the barn.

In her opinion, there was more to dislike than like about Nelson McKade. She'd known him only a few hours, but she'd learned enough to understand that if she kept him around for the summer, he'd prove to be a bigger pain in the backside than her temperamental cows or her rebellious son.

The fact that Nelson would rather be anywhere on earth but her farm didn't exactly endear him to her. And his fish-out-of-water expression as he'd watched her handle the livestock convinced her he seldom, if ever, found himself in a situation he couldn't control—a trait, coincidentally, she shared with him.

Still…she grudgingly admitted she'd felt a twinge of admiration for the guy. That he'd agreed to put himself through *rural hell* for his grandfather proved his loyalty and love for his family. And the gentleness of those big hands when he'd checked her face for injuries…

'Fess up, Ellen. The real reason you want to send the man packing is that he's h-o-t.

Handsome, sexy and so citified that the only business she had thinking about Nelson was to figure out a way to get rid of him.

Besides, Buck hadn't died all that long ago. They'd had no fairy-tale marriage—not bad, not good, just sort of there. If her parents hadn't insisted they marry and "make it right" after he'd gotten her pregnant, she doubted she'd have tied the knot with the man. Even so, the last thing she desired was the good folks of Four Corners snubbing their noses at her and Seth because she lusted after her hired hand.

At the porch, she paused to check her watch. Six-thirty—an hour later than their normal suppertime. Seth must be starving, unless he'd eaten the entire package of Oreo cookies in the pantry. Good thing she'd stuck a roast in the Crock-Pot this morning. She'd planned to make mashed potatoes, her son's favorite, but her feet ached and her back throbbed. Tonight, microwaved French bread would have to suffice.

The aroma of simmering beef greeted her when she stepped into the house. Her mouth watering, she bent to loosen her work-boot laces, and spotted Nelson's dress shoes on the rug.

The new hand must have noticed her meager furnishings—a threadbare sofa, torn leather recliner, dull wood floors, faded living-room curtains, chewed-up coffee table and yellowed lampshades. Most visitors would take one gander at the room and walk straight through the house with mud and manure slinging from their heels. Ellen's chest tightened with a hard-to-define emotion at the idea of Nelson, a man of obvious wealth judging by his car, showing such respect for her home.

Hushed voices drifted into the living room. Sock-footed, she padded across the floor and hovered in the kitchen doorway. Seth sat at the table, his back to her, and Nelson stood at the stove, frying…*hash browns*.

Having substituted a pen and pencil for a set of drumsticks, her son tapped out a snappy beat against the kitchen table. "How come Romeo's so messed up if he loves Juliet?"

Romeo and Juliet. She swallowed the laughter bubbling in her throat. She couldn't wait to hear Mr. Corporation's viewpoint of love.

"Because the love Romeo feels for Juliet is more like a hopeless crush," Nelson answered.

"A crush."

"Have you ever had a crush on a girl?" He glanced over his shoulder at Seth, and Ellen popped out of view before he caught sight of her.

"Sort of. There's this girl in seventh grade…"

Seth had liked a girl and he hadn't told her—*his own mother.* Another wave of guilt washed over Ellen. Any more guilt waves and she'd end up at the bottom of the ocean. When was the last time she'd sat down and talked with her son? Found out what was going on in his life?

Caught up in keeping financially afloat, she'd turned into a terrible parent and had neglected Seth's emotional health. For the past school year, she'd stood by the barn door and waved goodbye as he ran to catch the bus in the morning. They spent fifteen minutes at the supper table together, then he dove into homework and she checked the cows and readied the equipment for the morning milking. Often she didn't return to the house until after he'd gone to sleep. Weekends were a little better. Seth helped her with chores for a few hours before he spent the day with his friends. Why hadn't he mentioned this girl then?

Flipping the hash browns in the skillet, Nelson

explained, "If you've had a crush on a girl, you understand what Romeo is feeling. He loves Juliet, yet he hates her at the same time. She makes him happy, but it's a sad happiness. He believes his feelings are serious, yet foolish. She fascinates him and frustrates him."

"I get it. One day girls are all nice and everything and you like 'em, and the next day they act like they don't even know you and you get mad."

Nelson grinned. "I believe you've got it, Seth."

Her son appeared more at ease with a stranger than he had with his own father—probably because Buck had never made time for Seth when he'd been alive. He'd preferred the company of his fishing and hunting buddies to that of his own child.

Ellen tiptoed across the room, opened the front door, then shut it loudly.

"Mom's back." Five seconds later, the guys stood in the kitchen doorway, staring at her—Seth holding a pen, the hired hand, a spatula. Nelson's gaze dropped to her stocking feet, then shifted back to her face. His left eyebrow quirked. *Drat.* He assumed she'd been spying on the two of them. She flashed an innocent smile. "How's the homework going?"

"Okay." Seth nodded to his caretaker. "He helped me figure out how to explain Romeo's love for Juliet."

"*He* has a name," Nelson corrected.

Ellen stiffened at the reprimand. *She,* not a stranger, should be the one correcting her son. "Mind your manners, Seth."

"Sorry," the boy groused, then slipped back into the kitchen.

Nelson pointed the spatula. "Seth wanted hash browns."

The man should look ridiculous wearing her mother's ruffled apron with embroidered roosters on the pockets. Instead, all Ellen could focus on was how close those colorful cocks were to his...

Forcing her attention back to his face, she murmured, "I'm going to grab a quick shower." *A cold one.* In a flash she washed, changed into a T-shirt and lightweight cotton sweats, then twisted her hair into a messy knot and clipped it to the top of her head.

"I'll make the gravy," she announced, entering the kitchen.

Still wearing the apron, Nelson sat at the kitchen table, reading the newspaper. At least the cocks were out of sight. The only explanation Ellen could come up with for her lusty thoughts was that she yearned to get laid. She couldn't recall the last time she'd had sex, which had been well before Buck had died.

Hating how Nelson's presence unnerved her, she asked, "Anything interesting in the news?" She hadn't read the paper in months. Before her parents had died, she used to work the crossword puzzle while Seth ate his breakfast.

"Tech stocks are down again," Nelson grumbled.

"Seth, please set the table." Silence greeted her request. Before she had the chance to ask again, Nelson pinned her son with a nasty glare. Did the man expect to bully the boy into obeying orders? Unsure what to do, she held her breath. After a ten-second glare-down, Seth caved in. Ellen didn't approve of Nelson's intimidation tactics but admitted her son's compliance was a nice change from his usual stubbornness.

"Do you own tech stocks?" she asked.

He peered over the top of the paper. "A few. My portfolio's pretty diversified."

Lucky him. He had a portfolio. All she had was a bank account that ended each month in the negative column. Knowing little about stocks except that she didn't have any, Ellen remained silent and focused on the gravy.

"Would you like me to cut the meat?" Nelson offered.

Surprised by the offer, she uttered, "Sure. There're a knife and meat fork in the drawer next to the fridge." After Buck had moved into her family's home following their wedding, he'd never offered to help in the kitchen. He'd considered the house a woman's domain. She hadn't minded when her mother had been alive and had pitched in with the laundry, cooking and cleaning. When her parents had passed away and Ellen had had to add additional farm chores to her list of duties, waiting hand and foot on her husband had lost its thrill.

After setting the potatoes and gravy on the table, she glanced around. "No vegetables?" Her question drew blank stares from both males. Obviously, she'd have to watch their eating habits this summer. "Seth, you say grace."

"God, thanks for the food. Amen." He reached for the

meat plate, but Nelson's hand stopped him. "Ladies first."

She expected a protest; instead, Seth apologized, "Sorry, Mom."

That a complete stranger could discipline her son better than she could irritated Ellen to no end. She forked a piece of meat on to her plate and contemplated the word *lady*. She'd never thought of herself as a lady. A female. Woman. Farmer. Dairymaid. But never lady.

"The meat is excellent, Ellen. And your gravy makes my hash browns palatable."

"What's *palatable?*" Seth asked.

"Appetizing." Nelson winked at Ellen.

Winked?

Breathe, Ellen. Breathe. He didn't mean anything by it. She was acting like a foolish ninny...a...a... farm girl. *Which is exactly what you are—a dairy farmer.* A man like Nelson would never be interested in a woman like her.

It didn't escape her notice that Seth copied the actions of their guest—putting his napkin in his lap. Using both a knife and a fork to cut his meat. Chewing with his mouth closed. Sitting straight in his chair.

Maybe she ought to rethink her intention to boot Nelson McKade off the premises. Seth could benefit from the influence of a refined man. Good grief, Buck had never taught their son much in the way of etiquette around the opposite sex. How many times had her husband spat tobacco right in front of her face, or belched at the supper table?

Shoving his chair back, Seth announced, "I gotta call Brad and tell him I figured out Romeo's love life."

"Not until you clear the table and put the dishes in the dishwasher." Ellen flashed her don't-test-me scowl.

Seth opened his mouth, but Nelson cut him off. "We'd be happy to clean up the kitchen. It's the least we can do after such a fine meal."

"You made the hash browns," Seth grumbled.

Acting as if he hadn't heard the comment, Nelson instructed, "I'll rinse the dishes and load the dishwasher if you clear the table."

"I appreciate the help." Ellen scooted from the kitchen before her son launched another protest. She slipped her feet into her work boots, left the house and headed for the small pasture next to the milking barn, where the cows rested and fed on grass until the morning milking.

"Ellen, wait up!" Nelson shouted from the front porch, then jogged toward her.

Was he ever going to take off that silly apron? He looked like a clown, but she couldn't see past his handsome face to laugh at him. "That was quick."

"I told Seth I'd pay him ten dollars to finish the job."

"Pay him?"

"I assume he receives some sort of compensation for doing chores."

Without commenting, she continued around the house and down a path that led to the pasture.

Nelson dogged her heels. "Tell me he receives an allowance."

"He does not."

"Why?" His hot breath stirred the hairs at her nape.

"Because—" She stopped, turned without warning, and Nelson plowed into her. He grasped her shoulders, whether to balance her or him she wasn't sure. His fingers lingered, flexing against her collarbone. Caught off guard by the intimate caress, she blurted, "Because there is no money to pay him." *Darn.* She shouldn't be discussing her financial situation with a complete stranger. An *almost* complete stranger, she amended, since he'd just dined at her table.

"Listen—"

"No, you listen." Not in the mood to be harassed, she jabbed his chest.

His gaze narrowed on her finger.

"This isn't going to work." She poked him for emphasis. "You don't have all the answers." Another poke. "You don't understand what's best for my son."

Grabbing the digit, he held it prisoner. "I may not know what's best for Seth, but I sure as hell know when a boy requires discipline."

She gasped. "Are you telling me how to raise my son?"

"No. But whatever your method, it's not working. He's surly, disrespectful, lazy and—"

"How dare—"

"I dare because it's obvious by the state of this farm that you're barely making ends meet. That you're working yourself to death while your kid sits on his butt, talking on the phone to friends."

Ellen's eyes burned, not because he'd hurt her feelings, but because he was right. "If you're through lecturing me, I'd like my finger back."

He released his grip, then insisted, "I have a lot of experience running a business. I can help you get the farm back on solid financial ground and keep an eye on your boy at the same time."

"Besides the fact I don't approve of the way you deal with my son, do you honestly believe I'd trust a man who can't figure out one end of a cow from the other to handle my finances?"

"I don't see that you have much of a choice."

Chapter Four

"...climbed steadily in the early part of last week, reaching a high of 242 on Friday's open. Corn futures dropped lower, closing at..."

Ellen smacked the alarm button on the radio, for once eager to jump out of bed at 4:30 a.m. After a sleepless night filled with dreams—rather, nightmares—of Nelson McKade insisting he could fix her money problems, milking cows at dawn sounded downright exciting.

Swinging her feet to the floor, she sat up and yawned. So what if he had experience running a large business. Only Nelson, a man with an ego the size of his bank account, would assume that the challenges of an import-export company were equal to the day-to-day trials of a small dairy farm.

Nelson spent his day *bossing* people around, while she spent hers *coaxing* cows to cooperate. No doubt his employees dedicated their work hours to making him happy, whereas she dedicated her hours to making her cows content. While he wined and dined clients, she took food orders and bused tables.

The idea that Nelson believed he could devise a business plan to improve the farm's financial situation rubbed her raw like a piece of sandpaper.

Let him try, Ellen. What have you got to lose?

"Only my pride," she said to herself.

Her reasons for not wanting Nelson on her farm had nothing to do with his good looks, or his having made himself right at home in her kitchen or even his having won favor with her son. Her rationale was simple: she resented anyone believing she needed to be rescued.

Shoot, she was doing fine—

You're not doing fine. The ship is sinking...make that the silo is crumbling.

"Not true. The silo's tilting is all." With a little hard work and time, her finances would stabilize. The truth was she'd made some stupid decisions with her money since Buck had died and her naiveté embarrassed her. The thought of exposing those blunders to Mr. Finance made her shudder.

You mean the blunder where you canceled your health insurance this past January?

Without the extra income from Buck's paycheck, she couldn't afford the three hundred dollars every month.

I suppose you don't want Nelson to find out your VISA bill never slips below $5,000.

"Oh, shut up." Everyone mismanages money occasionally.

Money was the least of her worries. She was more concerned with Nelson viewing her flailing farm as a challenge—something to stimulate his mind and rescue him from the boredom of kid-sitting a teenage boy all summer. Before she left for the diner today, she'd make sure he understood he was to keep his nose out of her business. If he refused, then he could darn well find another farm to learn his life lesson on.

She padded across the room in her nightshirt, grabbed a pair of overalls from the hook on the closet door, stuffed one leg into them, then froze. She'd better wear a bra. Chances were the hired hand would sleep through the morning milking, but just in case he didn't, she didn't want him believing she was flaunting herself in front of him—as if one could flaunt a pair of breasts the size of walnuts. After dressing, she braided her hair and stuffed the long rope under a baseball cap.

Halfway down the stairs, she paused. *Shoot.* She never brushed her teeth until after breakfast. Heck, the cows didn't care if she had morning breath. She pivoted on the stair and rushed to the bathroom. There she cleaned her teeth, then checked for crusties—as Seth called them—at the corners of her eyes, before walking outside.

The moon, visible in the sky, illuminated her path. She didn't even want to guess how many trips she'd made to the barn during her lifetime. The hulking shadows of the cows loomed. She smiled at Betty's good-morning moo. As much as Ellen tired of this way of life, she felt a deep affection for her animals.

Inside the milking barn, she flipped on the lights and set up the equipment in front of the stalls. Afterward, she opened the pasture gate and spoke softly to the cows as they filed into the green barn. While the animals crowded around the feeding troughs, she put on a pair of coveralls and a cap, then washed her hands. One by one, she led eight bovines into the prep room, where she cleaned and sanitized their udders, examined them for injuries or illness, then hooked them up to the milking equipment. With a parting pat on their rumps, she reentered the green barn and began the whole process again.

The next time she glanced at her watch it was 6:00 a.m. She walked to the front of the barn and stood in the doorway, from which she had a clear view of the house. After a good minute Seth's bedroom light flipped on. She hated that he'd had to wake up in an empty house.

Sometimes she yearned for the old days, when her parents had been alive and her father and Buck had taken care of the morning milking. Back then she'd woken with Seth and they'd eaten breakfast to-gether—pancakes and sausage. Now he ate cold cereal and sat alone in the kitchen, with only the radio for company.

Today was the last day of school and she wished she could be at breakfast to share his excitement, in-stead of being stuck in the barn with the cows and...

Nelson?

Wow.

Wearing nothing but a pair of black, silky boxers, Nelson rubbed his whisker-covered chin. His hair stuck up in short spikes all over his head, his eyelids were puffy and he had an endearing pillow crease in his cheek. He appeared more human, more vulnerable than a man his age and with his temperament had a right to be. "Good morning." She winced at the breathless sound that escaped her mouth.

"'Morning," he grumped, rubbing his chest—his nearly hairless chest.

One of the cows lifted her head from the feeding trough and mooed, spewing bits of grain into the air. Ellen ignored the animal, unable to take her eyes off Nelson's chest. All that smooth, tanned skin…muscle…intriguing ridges and dips. Even his brown nipples were sexy. Buck had been as hairy as a grizzly, and she couldn't remember ever viewing his nipples beneath all the fuzz.

Nelson's brow puckered. "What's wrong?"

Nothing. She should kick herself for acting like a dope. She was a widow with a teenage son. The sight of a man's half-naked body shouldn't cause a ruckus inside her. She blamed her juvenile reaction on the fact that she was smack-dab in the middle of a sexual dry spell. "How did you sleep?"

"The bed's hard. The room's stuffy. And the pillow's too damn soft."

What a grouch. Hiding a smile, she added, "Seth starts the coffeemaker before he leaves for school. I'm sure it's ready, if you care to head up to the house." When he shook his head, she added, "He'd probably enjoy the company. Today's his last day of school."

He studied her as if searching for hidden meaning behind her words. She'd never been around a man who attempted to see inside her. One part of her found Nelson's interest flattering; the other part, downright annoying.

"I'll get my clothes and go up to the house." He disappeared into the small storage room.

Intending to be gone by the time he came out, she moved the final group of cows across the walkway, then paused in the shadows. A few moments later Nelson left the barn, wearing only his underwear and dress shoes, minus socks! Clothes stuffed beneath one arm, he marched up the gravel drive as if storming into an executive board meeting.

The mooing grew in volume, and Ellen had to force herself to continue her duties. However, she couldn't shake the image of Nelson in his boxers from her mind. What would it be like to be married to the man? He might be a big pain in the backside, but he was entertaining, and underneath his bossy attitude, she suspected lay a heart of gold.

Keep dreaming, girl. You've got nothing to interest a man like him.

As she rotated another group of cows out to pasture, she reflected on her marriage to Buck. Before they'd tied the knot, Buck had been happy enough to spend time with her. Then she'd ended up pregnant and everything had changed. Even though her parents had pressured them into marrying, Ellen had naively believed she and Buck had a chance at a happily-ever-after life.

Once Seth had been born, Buck began to change. Other than claiming his husbandly rights in bed—which hadn't been often—he'd distanced himself from her emotionally. Meaningful conversation had consisted of "Pass the peas" and "I'm driving into town. Need anything?"

Shortly after her parents had died, Buck had become much more vocal. Every time she'd turned around, he told her something he didn't like about her—her hair was too long. Her nose too big. Her hands too rough. She had too many freckles and she smelled like a cow. Then he'd tell her something she did that bugged him—talked to her cows as if they were human. Wore cotton underwear instead of silk panties. Dressed like a man. And listened to Elvis songs.

One day he'd returned from a construction gig and had insisted on a divorce. In a sense she'd been relieved. But her relief had transformed into deep, painful hurt when he'd accused her of holding him back from life. Accused her of being boring, uninspiring and a rock around his neck that threatened to pull him underwater and hold him there. He'd claimed he wanted a woman who wasn't afraid to live life—unlike Ellen, who hid from the world behind barn doors.

He'd left the next morning, and less than a week later, she'd received a call informing her that her husband had been struck on the head by a steel beam and had died of a massive brain bleed.

Burying Buck had been easy. Burying his painful accusations, not so easy. She wondered what Nelson thought of her as a woman. Did he find her intriguing? Did he think she was pretty?

What did it matter? The man was here for the

summer—if he lasted the three months. Then he was gone—back to Chicago, worlds away from her tiny dairy farm.

Noticing it was almost time for Seth to catch the 7:10 school bus, she unhooked the last set of cows from the suction tubes, dipped their teats in disinfectant, then pressed the chute button, releasing the animals into the pasture.

She was hurrying to the front of the barn, intending to shout goodbye from the doorway, when she spotted her hired hand on the cement stoop. Seth said something that caused Nelson to burst out laughing, then her son ran off toward the road.

Hand poised to wave goodbye, she waited for Seth to glance over his shoulder as he did every morning. She waited. And waited. Finally her arm went numb and she dropped it to her side. Angry, she glared toward the house, but Nelson had gone inside. No doubt he was sitting at *her* kitchen table, reading *her* newspaper, drinking *her* coffee! The least he could do was haul his backside down to the barn help her clean up.

You told Nelson you didn't want his help.

Well, she'd changed her mind.

Back inside the barn, she slipped out of her coveralls, then hauled the equipment to the washroom, where she piled it into the sink. *He* could clean the stuff.

All was quiet when she entered the house. Positive Nelson had his head buried in the stock market report, she padded down the hallway to the bathroom, intent on grabbing a shower. As soon as she flung open the door, her mouth dropped and hung crooked like a gate that had lost a hinge.

"You said I could shower in the house." He stood naked in front of the sink, shaving—half his face covered in white foam, the other half smooth as a baby's butt.

Incapable of uttering even a nonsensical sound, she gawked at his body. It wasn't as if she'd never seen a naked man before—just never one put together so well.

"For God sakes," he muttered, grabbing a towel from the hook on the wall. In a flash he had the terry cloth secured around his waist, concealing—in her opinion—one of his better attributes. She shifted her gaze to his chest in time to watch a water droplet roll down his smooth skin before disappearing beneath the towel.

"Why don't you take a picture? It will last longer."

When the sarcastic taunt sank in, Ellen averted her gaze to the can of shaving cream on the sink and resisted the urge to pat her heated cheeks. Slowly, as if she expected him to charge, she backpedaled out the bathroom. When both feet were in the hall, she leaned forward, grabbed the handle, then closed the door with a solid *thunk*.

Before she had time to skedaddle, the door swung back open.

"What the hell is the matter with you, Ellen?" He shoved a hand through his damp brown hair. "Look. I'm sorry. I thought you were going to be in the barn all morning. Next time I'll use the lock."

"The milking equipment is ready to be cleaned."
And you have a gorgeous body.

"I'll take care of it as soon as I get dressed."

Without another word, she retreated to the kitchen, leaned against the counter and covered her face with her hands. Sucking in a much-needed deep breath, she lowered her arms and glanced at the coffeemaker. A full pot sat on the warmer. A check of the sink turned up a dirty coffee mug.

Nelson had made a fresh pot just for her. She hadn't expected such consideration. Neither her deceased husband nor her father had ever made a pot of coffee in their entire life. Did all citified men know their way around a kitchen, or was Nelson the exception to the rule?

After grabbing a mug from the cupboard, she poured a cup, then collapsed on to a chair, relieved to be off her feet for a few minutes. The financial section of the *Daily Chronicle* lay open on the table. Several stocks had been circled in red ink and numbers scribbled along the edge of the columns. She leaned closer…*agricultural commodities?* What was he up to now?

"You should diversify, Ellen." *He* stood in the kitchen doorway, wearing stiff, brand-new jeans.

She'd just seen his naked body. More specifically, his *thing,* and all he had to say was she should diversify? She glanced at his colored dress socks, peeking out from under the denim. "You could use a pair of work boots. And some athletic socks."

"As I recall, there's a Farm and Fleet nearby. Seth

agreed to go with me after school. If it's all right with you, I thought we'd grab dinner while we're out." He paused. "Unless you have plans?"

Plans like in cooking...*not.* She remembered the half pound of deli ham in the fridge. "Nothing I can't change." She tore off a corner of the newspaper. "Write down your cell number in case I have to reach you."

After he complied, he pulled out the chair across from her and sat. "About the farm...I did some research on the Internet last night—"

"What Internet? We don't have Internet...do we?" Had Seth gone behind her back and actually signed up for service, as he'd threatened to do for months now?

"No. Seth said he tried to talk you into it, but your Amish heritage won't allow you to—"

"I am not Amish. I'm..." She snapped her mouth shut when she noticed the grin on his face. It wasn't any of Nelson's business that she'd told her son she didn't approve of the Internet rather than confess there wasn't enough money to pay the monthly service fee.

"I brought along my PDA. A device that's a combination cell phone-calendar and has e-mail. I contacted one of my executives and requested he e-mail information on the Illinois farming and dairy industry."

Good grief. She'd hate to have Nelson for a boss. "Aren't you supposed to be learning acquie...acquic—"?

"Acquiescence."

"Right. Is your grandfather aware you're bossing around your employees after work hours?"

He waved off the question. "This is different."

Arrogant buffoon. "You're not nervous someone in the office will tattle on you?"

"Not a chance. My team is very loyal."

The conviction in his voice convinced her he told the truth. She believed Nelson treated his employees with the same respect he demanded from them. In a way, she envied him. She wished she had someone watching her back from time to time. "Tell your henchmen not to trouble themselves collecting agricultural data. This is my farm and I'm running the show."

"Listen, Ellen. If this is a pride thing—"

"As a matter of fact, this is a pride thing. *My pride.* Leave it alone."

Expecting him to argue, she was shocked when he left the table and rummaged through the refrigerator. He set a carton of eggs on the counter, then removed a loaf of sandwich bread.

"What are you doing?"

"Making you breakfast."

Blast the man! She didn't want him taking care of her, too.

"What time do you have to be at the diner?" he asked.

"Eight o'clock. Don't forget the milking equipment has to be—"

"Cleaned," he interrupted. "Don't fret, Ellen. I'll make sure the job gets done."

Don't fret? *Yeah, right.*

"Anything else you'd like me to do before Seth returns from school?" He shoveled a greasy glob of leftover hash browns from last night's supper on to a plate. Next came two eggs over easy. A second later the toaster popped up two slices of bread. The perfect breakfast—for a truck driver.

"I usually grab a bowl of cereal—"

"As hard as you work, you need the energy." He set the plate in front of her.

"You're doing all this on purpose." She shoveled a forkful of egg into her mouth, surprised at the wonderful flavor. She thought she detected a hint of garlic.

"What do you mean?" He placed a glass of orange juice next to her elbow.

"You're being overly helpful so I won't fire you."

He tucked the edge of a paper napkin inside the collar of her T-shirt, his fingers lingering a tad too long. She wasn't sure if it was the feel of his knuckles skimming her flesh or the scent of fresh-from-the-shower man that made her shiver.

Then he playfully yanked her pigtail, whispering, "By the end of the day, you won't know how you lived without me."

Precisely what she was afraid of.

"YOU'RE DOING IT WRONG."

Lifting his sudsy hands out of the hot water, Nelson glanced over his shoulder, surprised to find Seth standing in the doorway. The clock on the wall read 1:30 p.m. He dunked the rubber tubing into the water. "Did you skip the last day of school?"

"We had early dismissal." He gestured to the tube in Nelson's hand. "You forgot to put the disinfectant in the water." He moved across the room and grabbed a gallon jug from the shelf, then set it on the sink. "Use half a cup. Soak the stuff for fifteen minutes, then rinse."

Nelson studied his already cherry-colored hands.

Seth rolled his eyes. "You're supposed to wear gloves."

"If you know so much, why don't you clean the *stuff?*" Nelson grabbed the jug, poured what he thought was a half cup into the hot water, then set the disinfectant back on the shelf.

"Me? You're the one getting paid to do this crap." Seth thrust his chin out—another trait he'd inherited from his spunky mother.

"For such a bright kid, you sure didn't learn your manners."

"I'm a redneck farm geek. I don't use no manners."

"You might someday."

"Yeah? Like when?"

"Like when you apply for college or go on a job interview."

"I ain't goin' to college, 'cause it costs too much money. I'm gonna be stuck here the rest of my life."

The defeated tone in Seth's voice concerned Nelson. "You don't want to be a dairy farmer?"

"Heck, no. I hate cows. They stink and they're ugly."

"I'm with you on the stink part, but Betty sure has pretty eyes." Nelson grinned, grabbed a clean towel, then wiped down the stainless-steel milking cans while the hoses soaked.

"Mom says the farm's my heritage, whatever that means."

"Heritage is important." Nelson got down on his knees and mopped up the puddles on the floor.

"I want a different heritage," the teen whined.

"Like what?"

Snort. "I don't care. Something that doesn't smell like shit all the time." His cheeks glowed red, but the boy didn't apologize for using profanity. Nelson let it slide.

"What if college was possible? Do you have the grades to get in?"

"I got Bs and Cs this year."

"If you earn As and Bs, you might have a chance at an academic scholarship."

Seth responded with another eye roll.

"Not as impossible as you might believe. Depending on the farm's income, and given the fact that your father's deceased, it's a good bet you'd qualify for financial aid."

"Lots of kids' dads die, and they don't go to college."

A pang hit Nelson square in the chest. "I can sympathize, Seth. Both my parents died when I was three."

The boy dropped his gaze to the tips of his sneakers. "Did you go into foster care?"

"No. Fortunately my grandfather was still alive. He raised me and my two brothers."

"Did you go to college?"

"I went to Harvard. Heard of it?"

The boy shook his head.

"The thing is, Seth, you can complain about your

life all you want, but it's *your* life and you're the one who's responsible for it. If you really wish to go to college, then you have to figure out a way to get there."

"You make it sound easy."

What could Nelson say? Getting into Harvard had been easy. Yes, he'd had the grades, but his grandfather's connections had made the application process a breeze. "Once you begin maturing—"

"I am mature." Seth lifted his arm and tugged at his shirtsleeve. "I got hair under my arms."

Nelson counted three, maybe four light-colored hairs. "Okay, so you're physically mature. What about up here?" He tapped a finger against Seth's forehead.

"What do you mean?"

"Are you making good choices? Are you being responsible? Are you handling your fair share of the farm chores?"

"I can't help with the milking, I got school. And Mom says homework comes first." He pulled the plug from the sink and gurgling sounds filled the room. "I work on the weekends."

"What if you planned your time better? Did your homework on the bus, then you could—"

"I hate it, okay? I hate milking the cows." He slipped on a pair of rubber gloves and began rinsing the tubes.

"You don't have to enjoy it, Seth, but you have an obligation to help your mother. No one gets a free ride in life."

"Yeah, well, if you had to milk cows every day, you'd try to find a way out of it, too."

Thinking it was time to change the subject, Nelson said, "After we finish here, we'll drive to the Farm and Fleet. I want to purchase a decent pair of work boots."

There was a long pause before Seth mumbled, "Sure."

"Is there a good pizza place around?"

The teen's face brightened. "Tony's Pizza Pub has the best pepperoni pizza."

"Good. We'll eat dinner there." Nelson headed for the door, but Seth stopped him.

"Can I ask you something?"

"Sure."

"Why are you really here?"

Remembering his promise to Ellen, he insisted, "I'm here to do farm chores."

"You got a fancy car and don't know nothin' about cows. You're here 'cause you wanna have sex with my mom."

Sex? That had come out of left field.

Before Nelson could respond, the phone on the wall rang. Seth yanked the receiver off the wall. After a mumbled conversation, he hung up. "That was Mom checking to see if I got home from school."

"Finish up, then meet me at the car." Nelson slipped out of the room before he bungled things and said something he shouldn't.

Sex with Ellen?

Okay, fine. He was man enough to admit that he'd fantasized about making love to her, before he'd fallen asleep last night. Hell, he had to imagine something pleasant to block out the bawling cows. Call him crazy, but in his opinion she'd looked damn fine traipsing around the farm in baggy overalls and a Tweety T-shirt. There was something about Ellen that stirred his blood. Made his pulse race. *But sex? Real sex? The kind without any clothes?*

No way. Aside from the fact that they'd just met each other and had nothing in common, he doubted Ellen Tanner was the kind of woman to indulge in a torrid affair.

Or was she?

Chapter Five

"Hi, Mom!"

At the sound of her son's voice, Ellen straightened behind the diner's lunch counter, where she'd been re-stocking napkins. Seth zigzagged through the tables, sporting a pizza-sauce grin.

Nelson flashed the same grin, minus the pizza sauce. Her heart did the pitter-patter thing at the sight of him. Aside from his good looks and nice physique, Ellen hadn't figured out why the man caused her body to short-circuit whenever he was near.

She stared at his feet. "I see you found a pair of boots." Danner boots, which cost two hundred dollars. That he bought expensive shoes didn't surprise her— he drove a car worth more than her farmhouse. But she did wonder if he'd checked the price tag before paying at the register.

"Farm and Fleet had dweeb-looking boots. I told Mr. McKade he should check out the mall," Seth commented.

Shrugging, Nelson insisted, "I didn't want to be a dweeb."

"Naturally." Her son had made the *dweeb* comment because he hadn't been to the mall in ages.

"I explained to the salesman I'd be working in hot, hostile conditions." Nelson grinned. "He suggested a USMC boot."

She glanced between the two males. "United States Marine Corps."

Seth praised. "They're way cool."

Ellen fought to keep from laughing. "You're going to war against my cows?"

"Hey, Ellen, how about a refill?" At the other end of the counter, a customer waved his coffee cup.

"Sure thing, Charlie." She grabbed the pot from the warmer and went to top off his mug.

"How's your day going?" Nelson inquired when she returned.

"So far so good." The way his brown eyes deepened in color told her he hadn't posed the question out of courtesy but out of genuine concern. Flustered, she checked her watch. "I get off—"

"Mom," Seth interrupted as he slipped on to the stool in front of her.

"Honey, it isn't polite to cut in when someone's—"

"Yeah, but this is important."

She motioned Nelson to the empty seat next to Seth. "Do either of you want something to drink? A piece of pie?"

"Coffee would be good," Nelson answered.

Ellen set a fresh cup on the counter. "Okay, Seth. What are you dying to tell me?"

"Mr. McKade says he doesn't want to have sex with you."

Like a deafening boom, silence exploded in the diner. All eyes—including Nelson's and Seth's—scrutinized her. She stared at the floor, praying the linoleum would curl up and she'd fall through a hole and disappear.

He doesn't want to have sex with me?

Surprised by the stinging sensation in her chest, Ellen scolded herself for reacting to her son's announcement. So what if Nelson wasn't physically attracted to her. It's not like she wanted to…to…do it with *him*.

Oh, really. Then why have you been daydreaming about catching him naked in the bathroom this morning? Ignoring the voice in her head, she grabbed a dishtowel and wiped furiously at a blueberry-pie stain on the Formica counter.

"You need to think before you speak, young man." Nelson frowned at Seth, then offered Ellen an apologetic smile.

"But it's true, Mom. I thought Mr. McKade was helping around the farm so he could…you know. But since he doesn't, it's cool. I don't care if he stays."

Good Lord. Why hadn't she noticed that her son had been concerned about Nelson living on the farm? And how long had Seth been wondering about his own mother having sex with a stranger? For that matter, when had the boy begun thinking about sex period? Good grief, she couldn't even remember if she'd had the birds-and-bees talk with him.

Then it's about time. She didn't wish for Seth to repeat her and Buck's mistake—expecting a baby in high school. Seth was a lot like her as a teenager. He hated living on the farm. Country life bored him. And he was getting to the age where he thought rebelling was cool. All those years ago, she'd felt the same way about her life and had been looking for excitement. She'd thought Buck was it. If only her parents had taught her the importance of using a condom *every* time. The proper use of birth control was one lesson she'd make sure Seth got an A-plus on.

Ellen felt like the worst mother in the world. Avoiding eye contact with Nelson and the other patrons, she grabbed Charlie's empty dessert plate, spun on her heel and retreated to the kitchen.

"I'm sorry, Ellen." Flo stood at the grill, a sympathetic droop to her mouth.

Ellen placed the dirty dish on the counter. "Sorry about what?"

"Your hired hand doesn't want to have sex with you."

"Oh, brother." She grabbed a dishtowel and began drying the cooking pots lining the counter. "I can't believe my son put me and sex in the same thought."

"You're a widow, Ellen, which means *you're* alive and Buck's dead. I'm sure you've thought about sex on occasion."

Ellen whipped away before Flo spotted her flaming cheeks. "Who's got time for relationships?" She certainly didn't. But she did wonder if she'd ever fall head over heels in love—for the first time in her life.

She and Buck had fallen in lust, which had fizzled out shortly after the courthouse wedding.

"I'm not talking about a long-term relationship," Flo insisted. "What's wrong with a summer fling?"

"You mean an affair?" Now, there was an intriguing idea.

Flo nodded.

"I'm a mother with a thirteen-year-old son. I have to set an example."

"I didn't say Seth had to find out." Flo flipped two burgers at a time. "Nelson is sexy and has money. One of those things must interest you."

She'd seen the sexy part this morning, and yes, ma'am, that did intrigue her. "Doesn't matter. He's only interested in one thing—my dire finances."

"Come again?"

"He believes he can reverse my financial situation."

"Exactly what is the guy's story?"

Waving her hand in the air, Ellen explained, "He's the head honcho of his family's import-export business."

"Sounds impressive."

"Yeah, but I have no clue what an import-export business does."

"If he's in business, he must understand something about money." Flo shrugged. "Couldn't hurt to hear him out."

Had her boss lost her mind? "What does dairy farming have to do with buying or selling…whatever it is that he buys and sells?"

"Nothing." Flo studied her with eyes that had witnessed more of the world than Ellen's. "If you won't let Nelson help, then maybe you ought to consider Billy Joe's offer to buy your place."

"I'm not desperate enough to sell the farm for below market value."

"Honey—" Flo's mouth curved in a sad smile "—it's no secret you're not happy. I hate to watch you work yourself into an early grave."

Was she that transparent? "Just because I'm stressed out doesn't mean I'm unhappy," she lied.

"C'mon, Ellen, this is me, Flo. You've always hated living on the farm. Why don't you let Nelson get you back on your feet financially, then put the place on the market and find out what it's worth."

Sell? What kind of a job would she get? Where would she and Seth live?

Then her deceased husband's voice echoed through her head: "That's it, Ellen. Stay in the milking barn and hide from the world."

Damn you to hell and back, Buck Tanner.

"Who is it?"

"Me. Got a minute?" Ellen stood outside her son's bedroom, staring at the Harley-Davidson poster taped to the door. When Nelson had offered to clean the equipment after she'd finished the evening milking, she'd decided now would be a good time to have that birds-and-bees talk with Seth.

"It's open," he called.

Drawing in a deep breath for courage, she entered

the room. Seth lay sprawled across the bed on his stomach, flipping through a video-game magazine. "Mind if I sit down?" she asked.

He scooted over, making room for her at the bottom of the double bed. Not sure how or where to begin, Ellen studied the size-nine foot hanging off the end of the mattress. Her baby was growing up too fast.

"Are you mad at me 'cause I said Mr. McKade didn't want to have sex with you?"

Leave it to a teen to cut right to the heart of the matter. "No, I'm not mad." Embarrassed, humiliated and a million other things, but not mad. "Although you could have picked a more private place to drop a bomb like that."

"Sorry." He offered a dopey smile and her heart turned to mush.

"Forgiven."

"Mom, can I ask you something without you getting all mad and stuff?" He dropped the magazine over the edge of the bed, where it landed on a pile of dirty T-shirts and jeans.

What did he mean by *stuff*? Unless he expected her to have a hissy fit or a meltdown. "Ask away."

"Did you want to have sex with Mr. McKade? Is that why you hired someone who doesn't know anything about cows?"

She'd intended to discuss sex and Seth, not sex and *her*. Ignoring the urge to run, she answered, "I hired Mr. McKade to help with chores, nothing more. Why would you even think such a thing?"

"I know you didn't love Dad." He fingered the edge of a tear in the knee of his jeans.

A gasp crawled up Ellen's throat, but she caught it before it had a chance to escape her mouth.

Seth rolled off the bed and went to stand in front of the window.

"Don't look all shocked, Mom. It's not like you and Dad ever kissed or hugged in front of me. And you guys never went out on dates like Brad's parents do. Sometimes they even stay overnight at hotels." He jabbed his big toe against the edge of the rug and studied the floor. "Did you guys have to get married 'cause of me?"

She'd never suspected her and Buck's relationship had been transparent or that their son had been so perceptive. "Yes, honey, we did. I got pregnant with you when I was seventeen. The beginning of my senior year of high school."

When Seth glanced up, his lip was quivering. She popped off the bed and hugged him. "It didn't matter that your father and I weren't totally in love with each other. We both wanted you from the very beginning."

Seth took a moment to digest her words, then his stiff shoulders relaxed. "If you could go back in time, would you marry Dad again if you got pregnant?"

"Absolutely," she answered without hesitation. "We may not have loved each other passionately—" *or at all* "—but I respected your father for not turning his back on you or me."

"If he hadn't died, would you guys have stayed married forever?"

Ellen recalled the cash that she'd saved over the past thirteen years, hidden in the living-room desk. "I don't know, Seth."

"You gonna get married again?"

"I'm not sure. Why?"

His eyes teared. "I don't want to be a farmer and live here the rest of my life."

"Oh, sweetie." She hugged him closer. "You don't have to be a farmer."

"But you'll be all alone. If you don't get married again, who's gonna help with the cows?" He wiggled against her and she released him.

"I'll manage. Maybe someday I'll try to do something different." *That is, if I can find the courage to walk away from the only thing I've ever done.* "Have you considered what you might like to do after you graduate from high school?"

"Maybe something with computers. I bet I could find a job in Chicago. You could, too."

Her insides twisted as she gazed into her son's innocent blue eyes—eyes that begged her to fix his world and make his dreams come true. He asked the impossible of her. How could she help him realize his dreams, when she was terrified to reach out for her own?

"I'm glad you're thinking about the future, honey. Remember, a lot can happen between now and graduation."

"Can I call Brad and talk about this new game I saw in the magazine?"

So much for the sex chat she'd planned. "Sure." She stole one more hug and whispered, "I love you, Seth."

"Me, too, Mom."

After Ellen left the room and shut the door, she collapsed against the Harley poster and rubbed her eyes. She felt emotionally gutted. She could think of a better way to end the day than being reminded of her inadequacies and fears.

She'd suspected for a long time that her son disliked living on the farm. If they moved tomorrow, he'd miss his friends but little else. She wished she hadn't gone to his room tonight. Now that his discontent stood out in the open between them, she couldn't very well continue to ignore it as she had the past few years.

But sell the farm? She was a single mother. Keeping a roof over Seth's head, food in his stomach, clothes on his back and a hundred other things he needed throughout the year was an intimidating responsibility for a woman who'd only ever milked cows all her life. Aside from waitress work, or maybe factory work, Ellen wasn't qualified for any decent-paying jobs. God help her if she were forced to choose between the farm and her son.

"Hey, Ellen," Nelson called.

Her eyes popped open and she rolled her head sideways. He stood at the end of the hall, a broad shoulder propped against the wall. He cocked his head and a lock of dark hair fell across his brow. Without even trying, he made her stomach drop and her thoughts scatter like seeds in the wind. When she noticed his red hands, she bit her lip to keep from smiling.

"What?" His husky voice carried a hint of intimacy.

"Your hands."

He held them out in front of him. "What about my hands?"

"First time I've caught a man with dishpan hands."

"The gloves make my skin itch," he said matter-of-factly, as if he submerged his hands in scalding water and disinfectant every day. "You got a minute?"

A minute. An hour. A day. However long you... Startled by her complete loss of good judgment, she shook her head.

"You don't have time to talk?"

"I mean, yes." Flustered, she added, "Let's go outside." The fresh air would clear her head and cool her body.

When she arrived at the end of the hall, he didn't budge, forcing her to turn sideways in order to avoid touching his body. On the front stoop, she sucked in a lungful of moist evening air, while Nelson stood at her side in silence. She drew in a second deep breath. This time a trace of masculine cologne mingled with the smell of damp earth. Why hadn't she thought to buy Buck cologne for Christmas? She'd always gotten him something practical like tools, a new coat or shells for his shotgun.

"There's a swing under the tree." Before she reached the bottom step, Nelson set his hand at her elbow, steadying her as they made their way across the yard to the ancient maple. His gallantry was unnecessary, but a balm to her feminine soul.

She couldn't recall the last time she'd sought refuge beneath the maple's giant limbs. During the summer months when Seth had been a toddler, she'd rocked him to sleep in the swing. Buck had believed the ritual foolish, but Ellen had enjoyed the quiet time with her son and her dreams.

"I never noticed how big this tree is," Nelson commented, shortening his stride to match hers.

"My great-grandfather planted the sapling in 1905 after he bought the farm." At the swing, Ellen brushed off the seat, then wiggled into a comfortable position at one end.

Before Nelson added his weight, he yanked the rusted chain wrapped around the gnarled limb. Satisfied the chain would hold, he sat next to Ellen and waited for her to push off. When the swing remained motionless, he glanced at her feet—the tips of her toes barely grazed the grass. "Want me to push, shorty?"

"Ha, ha. I'd like to see you struggle through life at five-four."

Grinning, he rocked the balls of his feet against the ground. She didn't have to convince him her height, or lack of it, was a handicap on a farm. Only an ongoing miracle prevented her from being crushed or trampled by one of her beloved bovines. It was a humbling experience for a man of his stature to witness this petite woman handle a cow with ease and efficiency. Hell, half the men who worked for him didn't have an ounce of Ellen's strength, stamina or guts. He wondered if her deceased husband had admired those traits in her.

"How did your husband die?" *Silence.* "Sorry, that was a little blunt."

"It's okay." A soft sigh drifted past his ear.

The vulnerable sound made Nelson want to hug her and promise to fix her broken world.

"Buck assumed he was invincible. Never wore a seat belt. Never wore a helmet when he drove the ATV. The helmet thing did him in. Unfortunately he wasn't wearing his construction hard hat when a steel beam clunked him on the head. And since Buck knowingly broke the hard hat rule, suing was out of the question."

"I'm sorry."

"It was bound to happen sooner or later."

The lack of emotion in her voice surprised Nelson and made him question her relationship with her husband. Time to change the subject. "What's Seth up to?"

"He's talking to Brad on the phone."

Fighting a feeling of restlessness, Nelson closed his eyes and sniffed the breeze disturbing the air beneath the tree canopy. Relaxing wasn't in his nature, and he itched to do something—anything but sit still.

Ellen suffered the same malady. She shifted around until she found a comfortable position—head resting against the back of the swing, tips of her shoes dangling in the air.

The night shadows allowed him to catch only glimpses of her expression. First, the tilt of her mouth as if she were dreaming of something pleasant. Next, a tiny frown line between her eyebrows. What was going on in that cute little head of hers?

He fingered the end of one red ribbon hanging limp from a crooked pigtail. Any other female Ellen's age would look ridiculous wearing pigtails. But not her.

Fanny Farmer was a very unusual woman. Unfortunately, an unusual woman with not so unusual money problems. "Ellen, I believe I can change your financial situation."

In one second flat, her posture went from slouched to ramrod straight. "Give it a break, Nelson. You're not sticking your nose into my business and that's final."

"But—"

"You're clueless when it comes to dairy farming. You've been here a grand total of two days and already you think you're an expert on cows."

"I've studied the dairy industry numbers for this region and I believe you can expand your operation without a substantial initial investment on your part."

Her mouth opened. Then shut. Then opened. "Look, Nelson. I admire you for jumping headfirst into something you don't have a clue about." A gust of agitated air left her lungs. "Obviously you're a man used to running the show. But my farm is one show you're not going to run."

If she'd give him a chance to explain, she'd see how sound his idea was. "I've done the research."

"Maybe. But unless you've lived the life of a farmer you can't grasp how varying issues affect the success of a farm. Weather, insects, fluctuating feed prices, disease, equipment failure, milk trucking costs, electricity and a million other things have to be factored into the equation."

"Okay, so there may be unforeseen circumstances. Doesn't mean there isn't a better way—"

"There's only one way—my way." She inched toward the edge of the seat, but he clamped his fingers around her wrist, and she froze.

"What are you afraid of, Ellen?" He grasped her chin gently and forced her to make eye contact with him. "Tell me your fears, then I'll take those into account when I come up with a plan of attack."

"I'm not afraid." She swung her head sideways, whacking him in the face with a pigtail. "I'm cautious."

Cautious? More like *stubborn*. "Nothing wrong with being careful as long as you don't let it get in the way of opportunity."

"You're talking in circles. What opportunity are you referring to?"

Finally, an opening. "You have to expand your herd, hire additional help and increase your milk production in order to regain your financial footing. In other words, you have to spend money to make money."

"I can't afford to spend money I don't have."

"You can't afford *not* to spend the money, Ellen." When she didn't interrupt, he added, "I took the liberty of studying the financial statements you left lying on the kitchen counter today."

"You what?" The words rolled out flat and cold.

"You're behind on your taxes—"

"Three months. Big deal."

"The minimum payment on your credit card barely covers the finance charge."

Her slim shoulders lifted, then sank in defeat. "I had to replace the blowers in the barn this past fall."

"If you continue to operate the way you are now, you'll be bankrupt in four years."

"Four years? How did you figure that time frame?"

"I ran a market analysis on the farm. Using the last tax statement, I factored in inflation, the cost of maintaining or replacing equipment and general bills and living expenses. I also added in a wage increase at the diner anticipating that you'd continue to work two jobs."

He paused, allowing her to absorb what he'd said, then explained, "In simple terms, Ellen, the money going out is greater than the money coming in."

"I'm curious, Nelson. Do you have a finance degree?"

"I have a business degree."

"How high is your IQ?"

Oh, hell. Why did she have to go and ask that question? Only he and his grandfather and, of course, test administrators knew Nelson's intelligence quotient. It wasn't any of Ellen's business, but for some damn reason he couldn't lie to her. "High."

"How high?"

He hesitated, not wanting her to see him as different or brainy. He wanted her to see him as a man. "One hundred and fifty."

Ellen remained silent, which bothered him almost as much as if she'd made a snide remark about his intelligence. "Aren't you going to say something?" he asked.

"What made you decide to go into the import-export business?"

The question surprised him. "What do you mean?"

"You have the intelligence to be a rocket scientist, to work at NASA, to…I don't know, find the cure for cancer. But you chose to buy and sell stuff?"

Not exactly how he'd describe his job. "I was three when my parents and grandmother died in a private plane crash. My grandfather raised my brothers and me. As the eldest I was groomed to manage the family business and make sure it thrived and supported my brothers."

Her callused fingers moved in tiny circles against his arm, setting off a sensory explosion beneath his skin. He hadn't expected her comfort, but appreciated it.

"When you were a little boy, what did you dream of being?"

"A fireman."

Grinning, she said, "Not too late to switch careers."

"I doubt my grandfather would be too pleased." Refusing to allow Ellen to change the subject, he insisted, "We were discussing you and your money troubles."

"Nelson, I don't have to be told I'm on shaky ground regarding my finances."

"Then let me develop a fiscal plan. You don't have to use my advice, but at least you'll have all the facts and figures in front of you."

"I hired you to watch Seth and do a few chores this summer, not be my accountant."

"I'll make sure Seth toes the line. As a matter of fact, he should be helping out around here a lot more than he is."

"I won't let you work him too hard. He deserves to have fun this summer."

"Are you speaking from experience?"

"Let's just say kids can get into trouble and rebel if they're pushed beyond their limits."

Nelson suspected Ellen spoke from experience. "Understood."

When she would have risen, he rushed on. "There's one more thing."

"All right already," she huffed. "You have my permission to snoop through my financial documents until your heart's content."

"Thanks, but I wasn't referring to that."

She tilted her head, waiting for him to continue.

"About Seth's comment in the diner this afternoon."

"Forget about it. I'm used to kids speaking their minds."

His knee bumped her thigh and heat raced up his leg. He set his hand on her shoulder and massaged her muscle. And it was definitely muscle. Muscle used to lug the heavy milk canisters in the barn. He pictured her firm, petite body under his much larger one. Skin to skin. What would her touches feel like? Was she an aggressive lover—strong, a little wild? Or was she gentle?

"Seth got it wrong, Ellen." He slid his hand across her nape and leaned nearer. Couldn't help it. Her scent, her softness drew him. She was an amazing woman. A widow who ran a dairy farm, worked a second job and was raising a son. The urge to protect her hit him in the stomach with the force of a roundhouse punch.

"Got what wrong?" Her breath sighed across his cheek.

"Got *this* wrong." He cupped her jaw, angled her mouth slightly upward and lowered his head. The barest caress…feather light. Then he retreated. "I've wanted to do that from the moment I hit you in the nose with the door at the diner."

He waited for some kind of response from her—a sigh, a laugh, a curse. Nothing. Had he imagined the way she'd gawked at his naked body in the bathroom yesterday? Was this attraction all one-sided—his side? Maybe it was too soon for her—a widow, barely a year. Cursing his insensitivity, he muttered, "I stepped out of line—"

"No, you didn't."

This time he kissed her the way he had in his dream last night. Open-mouthed. Tongues dancing. Teeth nipping. She tasted sweet and pure with just a hint of cinnamon-flavored toothpaste.

Ellen's mouth was eager, clumsy and inexperienced, but she made up for it in enthusiasm. With persistent patience he cataloged her sighs, her moans of pleasure.

"Ellen…" Never had a woman's kiss reached deep inside him the way hers had. She made him *feel… yearn…need.* His body trembled with an urgency that hinted at recklessness. He ended the kiss and pressed his forehead against her brow, struggling to catch more than his breath. "I didn't mean to get carried away."

"*We* got carried away," she corrected, weaving a finger through his hair.

He liked that Ellen wasn't afraid to admit she'd enjoyed the kiss. "About what Seth said this afternoon in the diner."

"Shh." The finger in his hair moved to his lips.

He couldn't resist. He sucked the tip of it inside his mouth.

"No more talk, Nelson. Not tonight." She pulled her finger free, rubbing the moistness against his lip. "Give me fifteen minutes and then the bathroom is yours." She slipped off the swing and headed to the house.

"You're sure about me looking into your finances?" he called after her.

The breeze carried her husky laughter back to him. "If it keeps you out of trouble, go ahead and stick your nose in my business."

Keep him out of trouble? He doubted it.

Not if t-r-o-u-b-l-e sported blond pigtails and baggy overalls.

Chapter Six

"Hey." Seth stopped in the kitchen doorway, yawned, then padded barefoot to the refrigerator and removed a gallon of milk.

"Good morning." Nelson glanced at the wall clock. "Nice to know someone around here averages more than six hours of sleep." Over a week had passed since he'd arrived at the Tanner farm. He and Seth had settled into a routine—Seth slept until noon and Nelson rose at the crack of dawn to help Ellen with the cows and with whatever other chores needed doing. After she left for the diner, he spent the remainder of the morning sitting at the kitchen table, studying tax returns, bank statements, bills and other financial records.

"How long you gonna work on that stuff?" Seth retrieved what looked suspiciously like a large, dog food dish from the cupboard.

"Almost finished." Nelson had been euphoric when Ellen had dumped ten years' worth of records on the kitchen table several days ago. The detailed documents allowed him to compare the farm's past financial situation with its current state. Not that there was much of a difference. Aside from a couple of good years, the farm had always run in the red.

Seth poured half a box of cereal into the dog bowl, grabbed the gallon of milk and mumbled, "See ya," as he went into the living room. A moment later, the sounds of a television game show drifted into the kitchen.

Nelson stood and stretched his aching muscles. For a man who worked out religiously in a gym, he sure as hell was sore all the time. Maybe tomorrow he'd take Ellen's suggestion and sit on the stool to clean the cows' udders. The constant bending over had to be the cause of his lower back pain.

After analyzing much of the data, he was certain the solution to the farm's financial dilemma remained the same—increase the milk production. He'd insisted that if she purchased additional equipment and hired more help, she could move twice as many cows through the barn in half the time. Ellen had balked, claiming a minimum of $20,000 would be required to construct extra stalls and buy extra milking apparatus.

He was positive more cows meant more income. He just had to figure out how to cover the cost of additional udder antiseptic, udder balm and a trillion *udder* things. Not to mention additional vaccinations, vet bills and cleaning supplies. He walked to the coffeemaker and poured the remaining sludge into his cup.

The past few days had been a real eye opener. He'd discovered that Fanny Farmer had no cash reserves.

No 401K. No savings plan. Not even a life insurance policy from her deceased husband. What kind of a man left his wife and son unprotected? All Ellen had to her name was the farm and the sixty-seven dollars currently in her checking account.

Regarding business decisions, he'd never second-guessed himself—until now. Four years on Harvard's crew team had strengthened his competitiveness and turned him into a poor loser. In his mind, *first* was the only place that mattered. He had a hunch that in order to help get the farm on track he had to secure an investor. The chance of finding someone willing to dump a truckload of cash into the day-to-day operation of a small-time dairy farm was next to nil.

What about you?

Ellen would never accept a no-interest loan from him. The stubborn, prideful woman would rather work herself into the ground than take a handout. Hell, she'd thrown a tantrum when he'd refused the small wage offered with the job. When she'd threatened to fire him, he'd had no choice but to accept the meager pittance. He'd then used the money to purchase cattle feed. If Ellen had noticed the grain barrels had been topped off, she hadn't let on.

Maybe she'd accept a loan if he promised to remain a silent partner. *You, silent?* All right, he'd have to convince her to take his money and his advice, but only for the summer. After Labor Day he'd pack his bags and return to Chicago, taking his advice with him.

You're joking.

Nelson ignored the voice in his head and gulped another swallow of muddy coffee.

What's in it for you?

"Nothing," he mumbled, then glanced at the doorway to make sure Seth hadn't overheard him talking to himself.

Liar. The real reason you're considering investing in Ellen's farm is so that it gives you an excuse to keep tabs on her.

"Why would I do that?" he muttered. All this manure-scented air wasn't good for his high IQ.

Because you like her. Really like her.

Okay, he'd admit to *liking* Ellen. What was there not to like about her? She was a cute thing with pretty blue eyes. And she was funny—sometimes. Determined, loyal and courageous. Most men would find a woman like that…*likable.*

There's more. She revs your motor.

Slamming the door on the voice in his head, he rinsed his coffee cup, then studied the one bill that had bothered him from the start. Something didn't add up on the milk-hauling statement and he intended to pay a visit to the company. "Seth," he called when he entered the living room. "Grab your shoes. We've got an errand to run."

The boy set the almost-empty cereal bowl on the table and vaulted off the couch. "Where are we going?"

"To pay a visit to Packard milk haulers."

"Cool." He raced down the hallway, then returned in less than a minute dressed in jeans, a T-shirt and untied sneakers. Poor kid. If a ride to a trucking facility excited him this much, Nelson could only imagine the boy's euphoria if he went to Disney World. Nelson made a mental note to try to plan a day trip somewhere this summer with the boy—a place without cornfields and silos. Maybe he could convince Ellen to allow him to give Seth a tour of Chicago.

Once inside the car, Nelson checked the map of Illinois, then headed west on RR 7. Packard Hauling was located on the outskirts of a small town called Farmington, sixty-five miles from Ellen's property. After making only one wrong turn, they arrived at the facility by one o'clock in the afternoon.

He parked in front of the cement-block building with the neon Office sign in the front window. Seth accompanied him inside, where a *ding-dong* announced their entry.

"Be right there," a feminine voice called. A moment later a teenager with flaming red hair stepped around the corner. "Oh, hi."

Nelson grinned at Seth's slack-jawed stare. The boy's gaze was glued to the girl's buxom chest. If Seth didn't close his mouth soon, drool would leak out the corners.

"I'm Nelson McKade. I'd like to speak with the manager or owner of the company."

"That would be my dad. He's down with the trucks. I can ring his cell and have him come up to the office."

"Don't bother. I'll find him." Because he wasn't sure how much Ellen had told her son about the farm's money troubles, he didn't want to chance Seth overhearing something that might upset him. "Stay here. I won't be long."

"Sure." Seth flashed a grateful smile.

Swallowing a chuckle, Nelson left the office, thinking it hadn't been all that long ago that he'd been thirteen and fascinated by breasts. He followed the gravel drive to the transport trucks parked behind a chain-link fence topped with razor wire.

A short, stocky man stood near the engine of one of the trucks, scribbling on a clipboard. He must have heard Nelson's footsteps, because he glanced up, then shouted, "Can I help you?"

"I'm looking for the owner."

"I'm your man. Russ Packard." He held out his hand.

"Nelson McKade. Pleasure to meet you." Obviously, the young girl in the office had inherited the red hair from her father. Russ Packard was as bald as a billiard ball but sported a crimson beard Santa Claus would be envious of. "Wonder if I could ask a few questions about your business?"

"You a government inspector?"

"No. I work for Ellen Tanner of Tanner Farm in Four Corners." No sense telling the man he was only there for the summer.

"Yeah, I know Ellen. We pick up her milk a few times a week."

"That's what I want to speak to you about. You're charging her fifty-four cents per one hundred pounds of milk weight to haul her product to the processing plant. After checking with other hauling companies, I find your price exorbitant."

"Wait just a minute, pal. I don't like what you're insinuating."

"The other haulers charge anywhere from seventeen to thirty cents. Why is Ellen paying so much?"

The top of the man's bald head glowed like a red stoplight. "Fifty-four cents barely covers the cost of gas and the hauler's wage to drive out there and get the milk. Never mind truck maintenance, insurance and taxes that come out of my pocket."

"I don't understand."

Brow scrunching, Packard studied Nelson. "C'mon. I want to show you something."

Nelson followed the man as he carved a path through the parked trucks and entered a doorway off what appeared to be a large garage. After flipping the light switch, he pointed to the opposite wall, plastered with county maps.

"Dairy farms are in pink, corn and hay farms in red and beef cattle operations in green." Packard motioned to a small triangular-shaped area. "Here's Ellen's farm."

The little patch of pink was no bigger than a thumbprint and surrounded by much larger areas shaded in red.

"Twenty years ago, the Bradford milk processing plant in Kentucky closed down." Packard moved his finger. "The nearest processing plant for dairy farms in this part of Illinois is now up in Peoria."

"Okay. You're hauling milk halfway up the state. I still don't understand why Ellen has to pay more."

"Because her farm is *way* out of the way. When the

Kentucky plant shut down, area dairy farmers switched to crop farming. Ellen's family didn't. Her dairy doesn't produce enough milk to make it worth transporting."

"You're providing your services as a favor, then?"

Packard nodded and tapped the large pink area north of Ellen's farm. "These dairy operations run several thousand head of milk cows. I leave two of my trucks on site 24-7. The milk is pumped straight into the tanks. Therefore, I can afford to give them a discount. Hell, the processing plant is only fifteen miles down the road from the farms. Ellen's cows don't even use a quarter of a truck's storage capacity."

Nelson was beginning to get the picture. He shook his head. Ellen would have to expand her herd to several hundred to compete with the other dairies. Damn, he hated admitting he was wrong. "Doesn't make sense for her to stay in business."

"I figured after Buck died she'd sell the place. With gas prices rising daily, there's going to be a time when I can't haul her milk anymore. Sooner than she thinks."

Nelson offered his hand. "I appreciate the information."

Packard eyed him suspiciously. "What kind of work did you say you were doing for Ellen?"

Nelson opted for the truth. "I'm helping with chores and supervising her son this summer."

The man studied Nelson's wrinkle-free khakis, golf shirt and clean dress shoes. "A friend-of-the-family kind of thing?"

"Sort of," Nelson hedged.

"Maybe you can convince Ellen to sell."

"Maybe." Nelson returned to the main office, where he found Seth sitting at the front desk, playing a game on the computer. "Ready?"

"Yeah, sure." The teen clicked on several icons until the screen saver popped up.

"Where's the office girl?" Nelson asked.

"Brittany went to get the mail."

"Brittany, huh?"

"She's way cool. She let me play games on her computer and drink a Dr Pepper." Once inside the car, Seth asked, "Why'd you want to talk to Brittany's dad?"

"For some information. Nothing important." The trip to the milk-hauling company assured Nelson he needed a new game plan. Truth be told, he'd rather face an angry mob of stockholders after company shares dropped than to try to convince Ellen to sell.

AS SHE HAD the past several nights, Ellen lay in her bed at the witching hour, staring at the water stain on the ceiling. She blamed her restlessness on the fact that she wasn't working herself into her normal exhausted state. Before Nelson had arrived to help with chores, she had ended her day asleep on her feet. She'd barely registered taking a shower and brushing her teeth before collapsing on the bed and awakening from a deep coma when the alarm buzzed before dawn—

A flash of brightness lit up the bedroom. Ellen rolled off the mattress and scurried to the window.

Someone had turned on the lights in the holding barn. Was something the matter with Nelson?

Refusing to analyze why her heart pumped faster than her milking machines, she fled the room. At the front door she stopped to slide her feet into a pair of rubber boots before heading to the barn. Outside, the glow spilling from the structure illuminated a path across the gravel drive, allowing her to move without fear of tripping. A gust of wind blew her loose hair about her head and plastered the knee-length nightshirt to her body. Holding the hem in place, she raced onward.

When she reached the barn, she peered around the edge of the door and sucked in a quick breath as a shadow passed along the far wall. Craning her neck farther, she spotted Nelson shoveling manure into a wheelbarrow—practically naked! He wore Buck's old rubber boots, black silk boxers and not a stitch more.

A smile played at the corners of her mouth, then faded when Nelson lifted the next shovelful of manure. The sight of all those sweaty muscles rippling and twisting wasn't a bit funny. Nelson had a dreamy body—the kind you'd see on calendars showing half-naked blue-collar men.

She must have made a sound, because the shovel froze midair and the muscles along his back hardened into granite. He checked over his shoulder, his face dark and stormy as if anticipating an attack. "Ellen? What's wrong?" He set the shovel aside and hurried to her. "Is it Seth?" he asked, tucking several strands of hair behind her ear. He did that a lot lately—fussed with her hair.

"No, no. Seth is fine," she assured him. That Nelson worried about her son made her yearn to give him a big hug. The musky scent of hardworking male swirled around her head. "I noticed the lights and thought—"

"Sorry I woke you." He plowed his fingers through his already mussed hair, leaving clumps standing on end. His gaze shifted from her face to her braless breasts, lingering a fraction too long. The simmering heat in his eyes sparked a fire inside her that erupted into an inferno.

"You look ridiculous," she blurted, embarrassed her nipples were flirting with Nelson.

He chuckled. "So do you."

"I guess." She plucked self-consciously at the front of her nightshirt. An awkward silence ensued. She broke it. "Seth said you paid a visit to Russ Packard this afternoon."

"I had a few questions for him." He retrieved his shovel and went back to work.

Edging closer, she insisted, "I agreed to let you view my financial statements, not harass my neighbors. I can't afford to anger Russ. He's the only one who'll haul my milk."

Nelson leaned on the shovel handle, his chest expanding and contracting as he caught his breath. "Did you know Packard barely breaks even with your business?"

"What are you talking about? I pay a fortune for his services."

"His fee doesn't cover all the costs of transporting the milk up to Peoria. He won't be able to haul for you much longer."

"He said that?" She studied the tips of her boots, afraid her face would betray the panic escalating inside her. Russ and her husband had been buddies. Evidently, now that Buck was dead, Russ didn't care to bother with her. Schooling her features, she insisted, "I'll find another company to haul my milk."

"Who, Ellen? You're the sole dairy farm operating in the area. Others changed over to crops years ago. Only the big operations can afford to remain in business."

"Good for those farmers," she spat, hating that she sounded like a belligerent child.

"What I want to know, Ellen, is why the hell you're milking cows instead of growing corn or hay? Better yet, why didn't your father or husband change operations when the processing plant in Kentucky closed down?"

"Leave my father and Buck out of this." Guilt churned her stomach. Her husband had tried to talk her into phasing out the dairy operation and switching to corn. He'd insisted he'd cut back on his construction hours and spend more time on the farm if they grew corn. She'd refused to listen, arguing that they'd go too far into debt purchasing expensive planting and harvesting equipment.

Buck had sworn he could find more land to lease that would pay off the equipment after five good harvests—the operative word being *good. No. No. No,* she'd answered each time he'd brought up the subject. Until the last time…when she'd reminded him the farm was hers, not his. The land belonged to her parents, and therefore he didn't have a say in how it was used.

Once tempers had cooled, she'd attempted to apologize, but her words had made little difference. Shortly thereafter, Buck had begun staying away from the farm for weeks on end. When he did return, he spent his time drinking with his buddies, Russ and Billy Joe.

"Ellen, something's gotta give," Nelson said, shutting down the memories. "You won't be able to hold on to this place much longer."

"Did I ask for your opinion?"

He set the shovel against the wheelbarrow with a carefulness that belied the pulsing blood vessel along his jaw. He moved in her direction, determination darkening his brown eyes to black. He stopped when the tips of his boots bumped hers. "Ellen Tanner, I have never had the pleasure of knowing a more stubborn woman. Half the time you're crazy, selfish and damn near insane. The other half you're gutsy, prideful and the most resourceful woman I've ever met."

She was so mesmerized by the movement of his bold, sensual lips that only the rich timbre of Nelson's voice resonated with her. His heated breath fanned her face as his mouth inched closer…closer…

He tasted of salt and frustration. His fingers flexed against her jaw, holding her head still for his gentle onslaught. Gentle turned demanding, his mouth nurturing the hot seed of need that had been growing inside her ever since his first kiss the night they'd sat on the swing together.

Sensations she hadn't felt in a long, long time…if ever…

He slid his hand along her throat, while his tongue danced at the corners of her mouth. Wet, warm, erotic…the reality of his kiss far better than her dreams. She swayed, her breasts brushing his sweaty, muscled chest. When she felt his hard desire pulse against her stomach, she flexed her hips and she and Nelson both moaned.

"So soft," he murmured when he cupped her breast. He grasped one of her hands and pressed it flat to his chest. Instinctively, she dug her short nails into the hardened flesh. His hips ground against her, the pressure sparking a blaze she was certain would turn her to ash in seconds.

Don't analyze. Feel. Just feel. She wiggled, aching for more contact with his body. Her breath, tiny, begging gasps of air echoed through the barn. Nelson must think her a horny widow. Wait. She was a horny widow.

Suddenly, his hands were on her hips, tugging her nightshirt up her legs. His fingers tickled the back of her knee, glided along her thigh, then snuck beneath the elastic band of her cotton granny panties. His mouth clamped over hers the same moment his fingers found the center of her heat. Stroke after stroke. Touch after touch. The chaos escalated inside her. Trembling uncontrollably, she lifted one thigh and rested her knee against Nelson's hip, opening herself wider to his touch. He slipped a finger, then two, inside her, and she couldn't catch her breath. Not that it mattered.

What little oxygen remained in her lungs was carried out of her body by her muffled scream as she pressed her mouth against his sweaty shoulder and shattered into a million brilliant pieces.

When she returned to reality, she noticed several things at once: she was snuggled against Nelson's chest, her cheek stuck to his sticky, sweat-slicked skin and her boots dangled several inches above the ground. Oh, and his rock-hard erection nudged her stomach.

Tears of embarrassment burned her eyes. Until now, until Nelson, she'd had no idea how desperately she craved intimacy with a man. Disgusted by her weakness, she shoved against his chest.

"Hey," he growled near her ear. "What's wrong?"

Refusing to look him in the eye, she muttered, "Nothing."

"C'mon. What is it?" His hands played with her long hair, coiling the strands around his fingers. "Talk to me, angel."

Ellen's throat clogged at the sexy endearment. Buck had never called her angel, babe, honey or even cutie pie. He'd called her Ellen…Ellen…Ellen. Plain old Ellen. After a moment, the lump in her throat dissolved, and she whispered, "I'm sorry. I don't usually act—"

He cut her off—that is, his mouth did. Slow and easy, with the barest hint of tongue. "Stay. Spend the night with me. Let me show you—"

She touched her fingertips to his mouth. Everything inside her screamed that she yearned for more.

Wanted Nelson. She was a big girl and understood he wasn't offering her a commitment. No forever. Just hot, sweaty sex.

Ah, Nelson. There was something about the man, about the way she caught him studying her in the mornings when she milked the cows. The way their eyes met and clung over the supper table when Seth chattered endlessly about video games. The way he insisted on locking up the house at bedtime for her. Nelson wasn't a man a woman had sex with, then moved on and forgot. She might be tempted to take a chance with him, but she had nothing to give Nelson save her body—which, according to her husband, wasn't all that terrific.

Deep in her heart, Ellen acknowledged that if she slept with Nelson, he'd leave her a broken woman when he returned to Chicago at the end of the summer. And she needed to be whole and strong, with her will intact to survive each day on the farm.

She untangled herself from his embrace, then fled the scene, not caring that she must look like an idiot, half running, half walking in oversized rubber boots. But she couldn't afford to slow down. Because one sound, one word from Nelson, and she'd turn right back around and take everything her greedy little heart desired—the consequences be damned.

"HEY, BETTY," Nelson murmured into the darkness as the hulking form of Ellen's favorite cow sidled up to the fence. He hadn't been able to fall asleep after his heated tryst with Ellen less than an hour ago. "I shouldn't have pushed her, old gal." He held out his hand, surprised the bovine nudged her wet nose against his fingers. The cow acted like a goofy house pet. He rubbed her head. She thanked him by blowing snot on the front of his shirt.

"I could have sworn she'd desired me as badly as I'd wanted her. Shoot, she'd crawled halfway up my body, begging for more." In truth, Nelson had been awed by Ellen's earthy response to his touch. He'd had plenty of experience setting off bells and whistles in women, to realize Ellen hadn't achieved that kind of satisfaction in a while, if ever. And he'd felt ten feet tall knowing he'd been the one to set her off tonight.

The moment had transcended the physical. There had definitely been more going on between them than kissing and touching. She'd broken through his emotional boundaries and set up camp in the vicinity of his heart.

"Next time I'll go slower."

What if there is no next time, Nelson?

There had to be.

She deserves better than a roll in the hay.

He couldn't argue with that, but he also understood his demanding career—excessive work hours and lengthy business trips—wasn't compatible with a serious relationship. He'd learned his lesson. No matter how much attention he showered on a woman, it was never enough. In the end, he and his significant other had been miserable and his job had suffered. He refused to take time away from work to fuss over a woman.

What if Ellen is different? What if she doesn't require coddling?

Even if she was willing to take second place in his life, she shouldn't have to. The best he could offer was an affair. And she damn sure deserved better than a summer fling.

"Affair," he muttered, the word tasting bitter in his mouth.

Betty butted her head against his shoulder, then ambled off as if she, too, were disgusted with him.

Chapter Seven

"You ain't got a lick o' sense. No one's raising dairy cows 'round these parts anymore," Billy Joe Plunket grumbled as he stalked Ellen through the milking barn, out the back door and into the adjoining pasture.

Sheesh! Couldn't a hardworking girl get a break? Ever since Nelson had arrived—eighteen days ago— he hadn't stopped harping on her about the farm. Now her neighbor decided he wanted a shot at her.

"I've got plenty of sense." Ellen had more brains than Farmer Plunket and all the men in Klayton County combined. Too bad she'd asked Nelson to drive Seth over to Brad's house this morning. She had a feeling her neighbor wouldn't be nearly as opinionated in the presence of another man—one with a brain, that is.

Ellen had been overjoyed when Brad's mother, Arlene, had phoned earlier in the week to invite Seth along with the family to a livestock show today. Seth needed the fresh air. A few days ago, Nelson had purchased a newfangled video game system and had hooked it up to the TV. Since then her son had barricaded himself in the house. Shoot, if she'd known what a competent babysitter a video game was she wouldn't have advertised for a hired hand this summer.

"Russ says he ain't gonna haul your milk much longer. And I won't wait forever for you to make up your mind to sell."

Ellen stopped at the huge aluminum water tank and picked up the large bristled brush near the spigot. She scrubbed the green algae clinging to the sides of the metal, thinking she'd rather be scouring Billy Joe's thinning hair until the last stringy strand fell out. "I don't give a hoot if Russ refuses to haul my milk. I'm not selling."

For over a year now her business relationship with Packard had been strained. She'd suspected he didn't want her business, but as long as he never said so, Ellen assumed he'd continue to haul for her. Now that Russ had publicly stated he'd have to cut her off sooner rather than later, anxiety was Ellen's constant companion.

"If you ain't gonna sell, then you oughta plant corn." He slouched against the tank, his spare tire nudging the side. "Your farm boy could prepare the fields this summer so you could put a crop in next spring."

Farm boy? "His name is Nelson McKade." She had no idea why she felt the need to defend a man she was spitting mad with. If Nelson hadn't stuck his nose where it didn't belong, her milk hauler wouldn't have gossiped to her neighbor. And Billy Joe wouldn't be yanking her chain right now. Why were men positive they had all the answers?

"What about Bones?"

"What about him?" Bones was the bull that serviced her herd. Ridiculous name for an animal that weighed almost two thousand pounds.

"You've had the bull four years now. You oughtta be worried about inbreeding."

"My herd is fine," she lied. Maybe Billy Joe was only a little stupid. She'd noticed evidence of inbreeding for the first time last fall when several of her heifers aborted in the early stages of pregnancy. She'd had to sell them off because she couldn't afford to feed cows that didn't deliver a calf.

"Buck was right, you know."

Ellen set the cleaning brush aside and faced her latest nuisance. He was several inches taller, but his beer gut would make him clumsy. If she fought dirty, she could take him down. "Right about what?"

"You're nothin' but a scaredy chicken." His beady black eyes flashed, reminding her of the rat she'd trapped in the barn last month.

"What did you call me?" It was because of ignoramuses like Billy Joe that rural folk got a bad rap.

"You're chicken to sell the farm."

"Ridiculous." Refusing to listen to the idiot insult her, she stomped into the barn. He followed, his stumpy legs pumping to keep up.

"If you ain't scared of selling, then how come Buck said you refused to move when he got a permanent job offer in Atlanta?"

She slammed on the brakes and Billy Joe plowed into her back. "What job in Atlanta?"

"Buck didn't tell you?" He whipped off his ball cap and scratched his oily head.

Ellen forced herself to act as if she hadn't a clue what her neighbor was bellyaching about. In truth, she remembered the night Buck had returned home from his latest construction job, adamant that they sell the farm and move to Atlanta. He'd had a lot of nerve insisting *he* had deserved a chance to live somewhere else besides the farm.

What about her? What about her plans to leave the farm, go to college and experience life in the city? Damn the man, he'd taken *her* dreams away when he'd gotten her pregnant.

She admitted it took two to tango. But Buck had been older than her by two years. He should have known better than to seduce a bored country girl whose one goal at that time had been to rebel against her parents and her monotonous life. And blast the man, he should have used a condom every time.

When Buck had insisted he'd deserved a chance to chase his dreams, Ellen had refused to listen. Everything Buck had mumbled about Atlanta had gone in one ear and out the other. Maybe it had been petty, immature and downright nasty, but if she couldn't have her dream, then damned if he'd get his. Come to think of it, that night was pretty much the end of their marriage. The next time she'd seen him, he'd asked her for a divorce.

"Buck said he could make twice the money in Atlanta, but you were afraid of moving to a big city," Billy Joe harped.

"Don't you have a row to hoe?" She trudged into the holding barn to check the six large barrels lined up along the wall next to Nelson's sleeping quarters. The feed in each of the containers remained at or above halfway. She hadn't purchased grain in two weeks. If she had to guess, she'd think a little—make that big— feed fairy had refilled the barrels in the middle of the night. Evidently, Nelson had to be reminded who the boss was—*again*.

"Ellen." Billy Joe spoke from the doorway, his mouth turned down at the corners. "Everyone knows Buck only stayed with you because of Seth."

She hesitated—her lungs half-inflated, her gaze frozen on the wall in front of her.

"Buck would've split long before he'd died if it wasn't for the boy."

So Buck had never gotten around to informing his friend he'd asked Ellen for a divorce. All this time she'd thought the locals had been aware of her husband's intention to leave her. Pride insisted she carried that secret to the grave.

If she kept her mouth shut, sooner or later Billy Joe would tire of carrying the conversation himself. But it irked something fierce that her neighbor believed Buck had been the one victimized by their marriage. "If Buck had cared so much for Seth, then why hadn't he stayed around more often?"

A nasty-sounding chortle burst from the farmer's mouth. "'Cause the woman he was getting it from didn't live on no farm."

"Oh, grow up. You think I wasn't aware Buck

screwed around on the side?" She'd had her suspicions, but until Billy Joe just confirmed them, she'd chosen to give her deceased husband the benefit of the doubt. More frustrated than hurt, she snatched the pitchfork from the hook on the wall and went in search of something to stab—preferably not her neighbor.

"If you knew Buck cheated, then why'd you keep him around?"

The poor redneck truly didn't understand much beyond the dirt he plowed up each spring. "I didn't care."

"You are one hard woman, Ellen Tanner."

"Best you steer clear of me, then, Plunket. I become dangerous when I get riled." She jabbed the pitchfork at him, grinning when he stumbled over his feet as he scrambled to get out of the way.

"Crazy female."

She held her tongue, hoping the pitchfork and her nasty glare were enough to scare him off.

"What's going on?" The question boomed through the tension-filled barn. Nelson stood in the sunlight pouring through the door, his hands curled into fists, his gaze riveted on her neighbor.

Embarrassment heating her face, Ellen lowered the pitchfork. Had Nelson eavesdropped outside the barn before announcing his presence? She pointed the weapon at her neighbor. "Billy Joe Plunket. His property borders my farm."

Nelson moved forward, his long clipped strides eating up the distance. He stopped next to her and removed the pitchfork from her grasp. Plunket's face lost its early-summer tan when Nelson didn't set the tool aside.

"Billy Joe stopped by to chat." Ellen added, "He was just leaving."

"I'm here to talk Ellen into selling out to me. I'd give her a fair price for the place."

"I'm not selling."

She expected Nelson to shoo her neighbor out the door but almost fell on her butt when he stated, "You offer fifty thousand over market value and I guarantee Ellen will give your offer due consideration."

"Now, wait just a minute," she sputtered.

"Fifty's a mite steep." Plunket rubbed his chin. "Would that include the cows and equipment?"

"Nope."

Of all the nerve… Was she invisible?

"Of course she'll entertain any separate offers on the livestock and equipment."

"Ellen will do no such thing." She stamped her foot, furious the two males continued to ignore her.

"What about the house?"

"Ellen keeps the house. You get first dibs if she decides to sell."

Hurt filled her at Nelson's betrayal. He didn't understand that she needed the farm. Didn't realize she couldn't leave even if she wished to.

Refusing to listen to the Neanderthals negotiate the farm's value as if it were nothing more than a piece of furniture, she stormed from the barn. They could bicker until they turned old and gray and she still wouldn't sell. All this pent-up anger made her thirsty. She sought refuge in the utility room of the milking barn and grabbed a can of diet cola from the minifridge.

Ten minutes later, Nelson leaned a shoulder against the doorjamb. "You're upset with me."

"You think?" She smiled, a nasty, bite-you-in-the-backside grin.

Anger sure looked good on Fanny Farmer. Pink flushed cheeks and spitting blue eyes. He wanted her in his bed. Right now. Angry, emotional, alive. Too bad he'd do her more good out of her bed than in it. "Plunket's right. You can't hang on to the farm forever."

She swallowed a giant gulp of soda, coughed, then hissed, "I believe you've forgotten who's the boss and who's the employee."

Although deserved, her remark cut deep. He and Ellen hadn't been acquainted long, but what they'd shared in the barn last week had been more, way more, than a groping match. He cared for her and her son. She had to realize that. "What about Seth's future?"

"Seth is my son, not yours. *I* determine what's best for him."

Her voice shook with distress. He closed the distance between them. Having to touch her, but understanding his touch was the last thing she wanted right now, he settled for straightening the straps of her overalls, allowing his fingers to glide over the gentle ridge of her collarbones. "Maybe Seth doesn't care to be a farm kid. Have you asked him?"

Her heartfelt sigh was answer enough. Seth had mentioned his unhappiness to his mother. Empathy, an emotion Nelson rarely experienced, tugged at his chest.

"It's only a matter of time before Seth rebels and chooses his own path in life."

"Speaking from experience?" Her probing stare unsettled him.

Crossing his arms over his chest, he insisted, "Myself, no. My younger brother, yes."

"What about your younger brother?" She offered her undivided attention.

Nelson wasn't proud of failing his younger sibling. "I ignored the signs of Aaron's discontent with his role in the family business. Instead of figuring out a way to help, I ignored him, assuming he'd adjust and settle down."

"Did he?"

"No." Nelson tweaked Ellen's pigtail. "Aaron promoted someone else to handle his duties, then created a job that better suited him."

"Wow. That must have taken courage."

"I admit I was impressed when I'd learned my baby brother had created a community revitalization division within our company." He grinned. "Without my knowledge."

"He sounds like a visionary," Ellen said with an unmistakable note of respect in her voice.

A stab of jealousy grabbed Nelson by surprise. What would he have to do to earn Ellen's admiration? "Aaron has definitely come into his own. He's engaged to be married soon and he and his fiancée are already expecting their first child."

"I'm beginning to understand—" she placed the empty cola can on the edge of the washtub "—the reason your grandfather sent you here."

Nelson cocked an eyebrow.

"The life lesson he wants you to learn…" She waved a hand in front of his face, almost whacking him in the nose. "It's more than learning to let others lead."

His eyebrow dropped back in place. "What do you mean?"

"Your grandfather was being polite when he used the word *acquiescence*." She poked a finger in his chest. "You're a know-it-all without a clue—the worst kind in my opinion."

He opened his mouth to protest, but she slipped around him. "And you have a nasty habit of bossing people around."

He shrugged. "In the end, I'm always right."

"Not this time. My farm isn't a corporation. Your Wall Street business strategies won't work here. If you can't respect that, then pack your bags and scoot on back to your high-rise office."

Ouch.

Even though Nelson admired the pride that lent Ellen strength and determination, he suspected her greatest strength was her greatest weakness. If she refused to put aside her smugness, she risked losing everything—the farm, the house, the livestock. Then what would she and Seth do? Where would they live?

"You want me to back off?"

"Bingo. If I make a mistake, then I have to live with the consequences."

He was an ass. Since the day he'd arrived he'd stuck his nose—make that his whole face—into Ellen Tanner's business. If she'd been the first person he'd steamrolled, he could have chalked it up to an innocent mistake. But for years now he'd treated others the way a military officer treated soldiers in boot camp—with no respect.

Acknowledging his fault only made the ache in his gut worse. Would he be closer to his brothers today if he'd shown more appreciation for their business input? If he hadn't been so quick to point out their short-comings or mistakes? Had his know-it-all attitude lost him his grandfather's respect—the one man he'd strived to impress all his life?

"I'm sorry, Ellen. I was out of line." Way out of bounds.

"Apology accepted. Now, if you're through pester-ing me, I need to check on Bones."

Typical woman—changing the subject. "Bones?"

"My bull, which by the way isn't half as stubborn as you."

"I bet Bones isn't half as good-looking as me, either."

"I THOUGHT HORSES were used to round up cattle." Nelson rested his hand against her lower back, guiding her around a large pothole in the gravel drive.

Nelson McKade was a true gentleman. If Ellen wasn't careful, she could get used to his simple cour-tesies. Shoot, Buck had never even held the door open for her. "This isn't the Wild West, cowboy. It's Illinois. ATVs in the summer, snowmobiles in the winter."

"Do you have an extra helmet?"

"You'll have to use Seth's." She opened the shed doors and removed a black helmet from a peg on the wall. She expected him to ask if she knew how to drive the ATV. To her surprise, he didn't. She backed the vehicle out and Nelson shut the shed doors.

He slid a leg over the seat, shifted one way, then the other, each movement causing her stomach to dip and quiver. Finally he stopped squirming and clamped his muscular thighs around hers, leaving no space between his *thing* and her fanny.

His warm breath caressed the side of her face as he leaned forward, pressing his chest against her back. "I'm ready."

"Hang on." She revved the motor, then shifted into gear. The machine sputtered once before jolting forward. Nelson's arms tightened like steel bands around her midsection, almost knocking the wind out of her.

"You sure you can drive this thing?" he hollered as she headed up the slight incline behind the holding barn and across a flat pasture dotted with an occasional oak and a broken line of hundred-year-old Douglas firs.

The farm had shrunk over the years. Past generations had sold off acreage to pay taxes and survive two world wars and the depression. The eighty acres left were plenty for running her small dairy farm. Billy Joe was nuts if he believed she could make a living off a corn crop on so few acres.

At the last second, she veered west, deciding to take the long way to the pasture where Bones roamed. For a little longer she wanted to enjoy the hot wind stinging her face, the sun shining in a near-cloudless sky, the heat from Nelson's body rubbing hers.

When a pond came into view, she slowed the ATV, then stopped near the water's edge. She removed her helmet, shielded her eyes from the bright sun and scanned the horizon. No sign of the bull. "The stubborn cuss wandered off his home turf."

Nelson slid off the seat. "Is that a problem?" He removed his helmet and hung it by the strap over the handlebar. He looked sexy in his stiff new jeans and straight-from-the-package Hanes T-shirt. Had it only been a few weeks ago that he'd walked into Flo's Diner wearing pressed slacks and a golf shirt?

"Bones never travels far from the pond. Most likely he heard the ATV and will meander back here in his own sweet time. Might as well soak our feet while we wait."

She didn't expect Nelson to join her. He wasn't a soak-your-feet-in-a-muddy-pond kind of man. So when he unlaced his boots, stuffed his socks inside, then dunked his feet into the cool water, she giggled.

He leaned back on his elbows, closed his eyes and lifted his face to the sun. "What's so funny?"

"You don't seem like the nature type." She swallowed a sigh of pure feminine appreciation as she admired his chiseled profile, his hawkish nose with the bump in the middle, his long dark lashes and dark helmet hair. Before she did something stupid like throw herself at him, she plucked a blade of sweet green grass and nibbled the end.

"This is the first time I've dipped my toes in pond scum." He opened one eye and stared. "Amazing what a guy will do for a pretty girl."

She rolled her eyes. "Oh, brother."

"Ever been to the ocean, Ellen?" He folded his arms behind his head.

"I've never gone in the ocean. But I saw it once from the highway when my mom and I drove to California for her sister's funeral."

"My youngest brother, Aaron, lives in California. He has a fishing boat we take out when I visit on business."

"Let me guess. Your grandfather sent Aaron off to learn a life lesson, too?"

"Yep."

Not caring if she appeared nosy, she asked, "What lesson was that?"

"Responsibility."

Something she'd learned at a very young age when she'd discovered she was pregnant. "What did he have to do?"

"He worked on a construction crew for a nonprofit organization that builds homes for the needy."

"Sounds rewarding. Was he like you?"

"What do you mean, like me?"

Fluttering her eyelashes innocently, she teased, "Was he as inexperienced in construction as you are in dairy farming?"

Nelson grinned unabashedly. "Yep."

"I'd like to meet this grandfather of yours. He sounds like a wily old coot."

"I don't believe he's ever been called a *coot* before."

"You mentioned your brother was engaged to his boss." Ellen's mind played with the idea of her and Nelson… No. *Never.* She wasn't the kind of woman a man dreamed of happily-ever-after with. "Have you ever been married?"

"Nope."

Rolling on to her side, she rested her chin on her palm. "Did you ever come close to marrying?"

"Once," he answered. "But she got cold feet six months before the big day and returned the ring."

Ellen couldn't understand any woman not wishing to marry Nelson. Except for his domineering, stubborn, macho attitude, he was perfect husband material. "What happened?"

He turned his head. "She figured out I was more in love with my job than her."

"Was she right?" Ellen wasn't sure she wanted to hear the answer. She'd never been Buck's top priority while he'd been alive.

After a long pause, he confessed in a low voice, "Yeah, she was."

At least he was honest. She should be grateful she knew where she stood—not that she'd even been in line. After Buck had died she'd made herself promise she'd never settle for taking the backseat in a relationship. But right now, hypnotized by Nelson's dreamy brown eyes, she wasn't so sure she could keep that promise if he offered her less than what she deserved. "Do you work long hours?" she asked.

"Yes."

"Do you *have* to work long hours or do you *choose* to?"

"Choose to."

The man took honesty to a whole new level. "What

does your grandfather think about your workaholic tendencies?"

"He believes I'm obsessive." Nelson sat up, pulled his feet from the water and draped his arms over his knees. "He celebrated ninety-one this past May."

"You're fortunate to still have him."

"I agree. Sometimes we don't see eye to eye, but he's always been there. I can't imagine life without the old—" he grinned "—coot around." After a long pause, Nelson spoke. "Can I ask you something, Ellen?"

"Sure."

"Does your deceased husband have anything to do with you refusing to sell the farm?"

"No, Buck wasn't attached to the farm." Or her for that matter.

"If you had a reason to start over someplace new, would you?"

"Maybe." *If you were the reason.*

"Bull," he protested, scrambling to his feet.

Bull? Ellen stared in the direction of his pointing finger.

Oh, *bull.* Bones had arrived.

The mangy animal had impeccable timing.

Chapter Eight

If you had a reason to start over someplace new, would you?

Too much fresh air. That was the only explanation Nelson could come up with for the idiotic question he'd asked Ellen a few moments ago. Now she'd assume he was romantically interested in her. He wasn't. *Was he?*

He studied her out of the corner of his eye and swallowed hard. She was such a contradiction from the women who usually made his head turn. And he wasn't referring to her short height, blond pigtails or makeupless face, all of which he wholeheartedly approved of. What really attracted him to Ellen was the idea that she wasn't afraid to stand up to him. For some reason that turned him on. Yet at the same time, it made him nervous. Nervous because she threatened his control. Forced him to question what he'd always thought he'd wanted from life. What he'd believed was important. Each time he gazed into her beautiful blue eyes, he felt himself slip. Struggle to recall why he'd allowed his career to supersede his own happiness. But his career and happiness went hand in hand. Or maybe not.

"Stay here. I'm going to examine Bones." Ellen struggled to shove her wet toes inside her socks.

He'd have to contemplate the definition of *happiness* later. Right now Ellen's safety was his main concern. "Shouldn't you put an animal that size in a cage before you go near it?" The bull could do serious damage to Fanny Farmer's petite body.

"Bones is pretty docile," she assured him, stuffing her sock feet inside the work boots. "As long as I don't make any sudden moves, he'll let me touch him."

"Maybe I should—" He stopped short at her scowl.

"Which one of us has more experience in this situation—me, Farmer Ellen, or you, Executive Nelson?"

"Are all country girls full of this much sass?"

Her scowl curved into a smile. "Best you stay out of my line of fire, McKade."

His first impulse was to ignore Ellen's directive. He put on his shoes, stood, took one step, then froze when his grandfather's words echoed through his head— *Nelson, you've become too adept at bulldozing people.* The idea that his grandfather, and maybe others, associated his leadership style with bulldozing caused an odd mixture of humiliation and hurt to congeal in his stomach like a mass of rotting food. Nelson had always taken pride in believing his decisions had the company's and his employees' best interests at heart.

To stand aside and trust that Ellen knew what she was doing was more difficult than he anticipated. This time, his urgency to take control did not stem from hating to follow orders but from fear—fear for her safety.

Nelson rarely experienced fear. If he did, he refused to acknowledge it. That Ellen brought this emotion to the surface troubled him. How could he return to his old life with Ellen and Seth's situation lingering in the back of his mind?

"What are you looking for?" he asked.

"Sores, infection, cuts, open wounds," she answered, her voice calm and quiet as she circled the bull. "Anything that might need medical attention."

Her head didn't clear the animal's back, leaving only her jean-clad legs visible beneath the belly. When she paused, his gut clenched. "What's wrong?"

"Bones is favoring his right hind leg."

Nelson's gaze zeroed in on the leg in question, but he couldn't detect an injury. He moved closer, then halted when the bull swung his head and snorted a warning. The animal's restless movements signaled that it was time for Ellen to move away. "I don't see anything wrong."

"He's not putting all his weight on it." She moved to the massive head and Nelson exhaled a gust of air, relieved he could view her entire body. With Bones's horns filed down to stubs, at least he didn't have to worry about Ellen becoming a human kebab. "Call the vet."

"The vet is a last resort." She had her back to him as she edged along the animal's flank, running her hands over the tough hide.

"Last resort?"

"The vet charges a hundred dollars a house call." She paused by the bull's rump.

A hundred dollars—pocket change. Ellen's worry over spending such a small amount brought to light the enormous socioeconomic gap between them. The urge to close the gap was surprisingly strong—an odd feeling for a man who'd always been more concerned with making money than doling it out. "I'll pay the vet bill."

"Thanks, but no, thanks. Would you fetch the medical bag from the compartment on the back of the ATV?"

Nelson hurried to the ATV and lifted the lid on the storage bin attached to the back of the seat. He just retrieved the pouch when, a second later, Ellen's scream rent the air. Ice-cold terror pumped through his veins as he whipped around and discovered Ellen flat on her back, clutching her thigh.

Without a thought for his own safety, he ran at the bull, waving his arms and shouting. Bones snorted, stamped his hoof, then trotted to an evergreen several yards away. Nelson knelt at Ellen's side, his heart banging against his ribs. "Angel, can you hear me?"

"You don't have to shout, Nelson. I didn't get kicked in the head."

"Sorry." He lowered his voice. "What happened?"

"Bones kicked my thigh when I removed a thorn by his dew claw."

"Does your femur feel broken?"

"I don't know. My leg is numb."

"Where does it hurt the most?" He wrapped his fingers around her knee and pressed gently.

She batted his hand away. "Stop hovering and help me up."

Grabbing both her arms, he hauled her to her feet, then tightened his hold when her face turned pasty white. "Don't faint on me, Tanner."

"I've never fainted in my life."

Less than ten yards separated them from the ATV, but if she couldn't feel her leg... "I'll carry you."

"No, you won't." She took one step and the smattering of freckles across the bridge of her nose vanished. When her eyes rolled back, Nelson sprang forward and swooped her up into his arms. *Stubborn woman.*

He carried her to the ATV, checking every few steps to make sure the bull hadn't moved from beneath the tree. Bones appeared more interested in grazing than charging. With care, Nelson straddled the machine and nestled Ellen in his lap.

"What happened?" she moaned, her head rolling against his chest.

"You fainted."

"Liar."

If she didn't look so pathetic, he might laugh at her bravado.

"Can you drive an ATV?" she asked.

"I'll manage." He stuffed Ellen's helmet on her head before grabbing his.

"Don't tip us over, McKade."

His heart clenched at the wobble in her voice—an indication she was in more pain than she let on. Because of her take-charge attitude and the fact that she was so capable around the farm, she appeared larger than life in Nelson's eyes. Never more than now—injured and huddled against him—were her smallness and frailty startlingly apparent.

"I forgot to mention something," she murmured.

"What's that?" He cranked the key in the ignition and revved the motor.

"Bones likes to chase the ATV."

"Chase the…you've got to be kidding." He glanced over his shoulder, surprised that the bull had moved away from the tree. *He can't outrun this machine.*

"Don't slow down."

Nelson glared at the top of Ellen's helmet and thought of his comfy office back in Chicago. How the hell had he lost all control of his life? "What about the gate?"

"If you open it, I'll drive through, then you can shut it before Bones escapes."

"Hang on," he warned. The ATV shot forward, almost unseating them both. The ride was bumpy as hell and he hurt thinking about the additional pain it was causing Ellen. Halfway across the pasture, he screwed up the courage to check behind him. The blasted beast was right on their tail, trotting damn fast for an animal with a lame leg.

The gate came into view not a minute too soon. Nelson stopped the ATV, hopped off, lifted the latch and waited until Ellen drove through before securing it. Sensing he was beaten, Bones slowed his pace, but didn't stop until he arrived at the gate. He pawed the ground once, then rammed his head into the metal bars.

"Poor loser." Nelson flashed his middle finger.

Bones snorted before ambling off.

Swallowing a mouthful of obscenities, Nelson hopped on the ATV. Now that they were out of danger, he drove slower, attempting to avoid the bumps and ruts in the ground.

He parked by the shed, lifted Ellen off the seat and ignored her protests as he carried her into the house. Once inside, he set her on the sofa and demanded, "Remove your pants."

"My pants are staying right where they are." She attempted to stand, but the moment she put weight on her injured leg, it buckled and she collapsed on to the cushions and moaned.

Ellen's courage humbled him. In great pain, she'd yet to cry a single tear. "Either lose the pants, so I can check your thigh, or I'm calling 911."

"Bully."

He reached for the snap on her jeans, only to have his hands batted away.

"Turn around."

"It's not like I haven't seen a woman in her underwear before."

"Well, you're not seeing mine."

"Oh, for Christ's sake. Since when do farmers care about modesty?"

She stuck out her tongue. *Brat.*

Assuming she'd injure her leg worse if they tussled over a pair of jeans, he retreated to the opposite side of the coffee table and stared out the living-room window. *And she thinks I'm stubborn?*

"I need help," she muttered.

"Can I turn around?"

"Yes."

She looked pathetic—a red-white-and-blue afghan spread across her lap, her jeans waded up at her ankles and her slim thighs, one white and one purple and blue, exposed. He schooled his features, not wanting her to detect how her condition affected him. How he wished he could trade places with her. Wished his touch could ease her pain. He scooted around the table and knelt in front of her. "Aw, Ellen."

"It's just a bruise," she protested, then sniffed.

He gently ran his fingers around the edges of the wound. Her leg felt too delicate to suffer such a brutal kick. "Bones may not have broken your femur but he broke plenty of blood vessels. A doctor should examine you."

"No doctor. I'll be fine after I ice my leg down and take some pain medication. The Motrin is in the cupboard by the kitchen sink."

The determined set of her mouth guaranteed he wouldn't win this battle. "If your leg gets any worse, I'm driving you to the hospital." He left her to stew on his threat and went into the kitchen. There he confiscated a bag of frozen peas from the freezer, filled a glass with milk, then retrieved the medication from the cupboard and returned to the living room.

"Here." He offered the tablets and glass of milk. After she swallowed them, he ordered, "Lie down." He lifted her legs on to the cushions, then removed her boots and socks before pulling off her jeans. Next, he stuffed a pillow beneath her head and placed the bag of peas on the injury. "When the peas thaw, there's a bag of corn waiting."

"You shouldn't waste food."

"I'll make a vegetable casserole for supper."

As intended, the comment brought a smile to her pinched face. "Seth will be thrilled."

"You want the TV on while I'm down in the barn?" he asked.

"Why are you going to the barn?"

"Milk the cows." What else did she think he'd do in a milking barn? He should check her head. Maybe she'd smacked it against the ground when she'd fallen.

"The cows can wait a while longer. I'll be fine in a few minutes."

Ellen was fooling herself if she assumed she could milk cows standing on one leg. However, she'd argue her way off the couch if he didn't give in. "All right." He played along. "You can milk the cows later. I'll make sure the equipment is ready to go when you are."

"Thanks." With an exhausted sigh, she rolled her head to the side and closed her eyes.

Nelson wasn't anticipating milking the cows all by his lonesome, but he'd manage. Over the past few days, Seth had showed him the ins and outs of cow milking and a few shortcuts Ellen didn't know about. He arranged the quilt over her legs, tucked the edges around her feet, then leaned over and kissed her forehead before sneaking out the door.

Jay Leno's voice registered in the back of Ellen's mind as she struggled toward consciousness. The opening theme of the *Tonight Show* faded, the TV's volume rising as a credit-card commercial aired. Her head felt like a supersize cotton ball—weightless and empty, except for the nagging thought that she never fell asleep in front of the television.

Her eyes begged to remain closed, and only her concentrated effort forced them open. She slid her gaze to the wall clock across the room. 11:00 p.m. *Seth!* Why hadn't her son woken her when he'd returned from spending the day with Brad and his family?

A wicked bolt of fire shot through her thigh as she swung her legs off the sofa, sending a thawed bag of sweet corn on to the floor. Teeth clenched, she gripped the cushion and pulled herself into a sitting position. She sucked in crisp gasps of air as her head threatened to float away.

When the agony settled into a dull throb and the red haze in front of her eyes cleared, she spotted a package of lima beans on the floor by her foot. Nelson had better not have wasted her entire month's supply of veggies on her leg. Speaking of the hired hand...he was stretched out in the recliner, sound asleep.

His big bare feet hung off the end, and quiet snores escaped his parted lips. In sleep, he appeared younger and less...less *bossy.* Although she had to admit that she'd appreciated his bossiness earlier in the day. Her lips curved upward as she recalled how he'd insisted on carrying her into the house. For the first time in her life she'd experienced the great feminine phenomenon of being swept off her feet—literally and figuratively.

Buck hadn't even carried her over the threshold on their wedding day. At eight months pregnant, she'd been as unwieldy as a cow. Still... Her teenage heart had hoped her new husband might view her as a treasured possession, not a responsibility. Ellen had learned quickly that her deceased husband hadn't been a man she could trust for emotional support.

At times, Nelson came across as hard and unyielding. But the gentle way he'd handled her, the concern that had softened his brown eyes when he'd checked her wound, made her believe he was a man who would cherish the woman he cared deeply for. She suspected his caring could evolve into smothering, but from where she sat at the moment...she'd welcome a little suffocation.

How easily she could waste an entire day analyzing the inner workings of Nelson's mind. But there were more important things to ponder than her hired hand—her cows. Had Seth helped with the evening milking? She couldn't fathom Nelson managing the small herd on his own.

Exhausted, she lay back against the pillow and stared at the ceiling, surprised to find another water stain overhead. She'd have to add a new roof to her growing list of farm repairs. Everything around her was falling into disrepair and she didn't have a dime to her name. A tear rolled down her cheek. Horrified, she rubbed the moisture away.

Crying was a waste of energy. Tears didn't milk cows, didn't pay bills, nor did they repair leaky roofs.

Feeling as if her life were spinning out of control, she dabbed her eyes with the corner of the afghan.

Damn bull. Bones had never hurt her before. She'd poked and prodded that darn animal too many times to count since she'd bought him. The blasted thorn she'd tugged from his dew claw had been small in comparison with other debris she'd picked from his hide. Maybe Nelson's presence had set the bull on edge.

What if Bones *had* broken her thigh bone? How would she manage the cows? Seth would have to take over the milking chores and his summer vacation would be ruined. She lifted the edge of the blanket and studied her injury.

The swelling had receded some, leaving behind a grotesque bruise. Streaks of black, blue and red fanned from the center of the wound, making her skin appear as though it had suffered a bad tie-dye job. She murmured a heavenly thank-you that Bones had missed her kneecap. A hoof there would have shattered the joint and crippled her for life. That was a sobering thought.

Her injury forced her to examine her situation long and hard. For the past few years, even more so since Buck's death, she'd fought the temptation to sell off everything. But the farm was like an abusive husband; years of milking cows and doing little else with her life had sucked her dry of confidence and self-esteem.

The fact that she wasn't qualified to do much else roped her to this meager existence. With no family to ask for help, it was too risky to begin again in a new occupation, especially when she had a son depending on her. If only Nelson's grandfather hadn't been the one to answer her ad.

Nelson made her wish more than ever that she had someone to share her burdens. Not someone—Nelson. How nice it would feel to rest her weary head on his shoulder each night, knowing he'd be there in the morning to help her face the day's troubles. She wished with all her heart he were *the one. Her man. Her haven.*

Even if Nelson offered her a future with him, she'd be a fool to believe the relationship would last. How could it? She had nothing to interest a man like him. Besides, she couldn't envision living in a big city like Chicago. Nope. She was born a simple country girl. She would die a simple country girl.

Before her heart took a tumble it couldn't recover from, she'd better put an end to any notion about her, *him* and a lasting relationship. She glanced at the recliner, hoping her sniffles hadn't woken Nelson. Fat chance.

Ellen drowned in the solemn brown eyes that stared at her. With just a look, this man could make her heart stumble.

Damn bull. If Bones hadn't stomped her good, she wouldn't be sitting on the couch, emotional and weepy and wishing she and Nelson were more than boss and employee.

Raising his arms above his head, he stretched, then without a word left the chair and padded into the kitchen. He returned with a glass of water and two pain pills. After he handed her the medication, he made room for himself on the couch. "Hurts like hell, huh?" He smoothed a hand over her hair.

Her eyes betrayed her and tears leaked from the corners. At least he'd believe physical pain and not emotional agony was tearing her apart. Nelson rubbed the pad of his thumb over her wet cheeks. His gentleness caused the tears to fall faster. And faster.

"Ah, babe."

Her heart sighed as his mouth drew nearer. How did he know she desperately needed a kiss—his kiss? Her lashes fluttered, then closed when his lips grazed hers. The firm press comforted, urged her to lean on him…for a precious few moments. He shifted, his chest rubbing her breasts, his solid presence reassuring and warm.

Without warning, he levered himself off the couch. Stunned, Ellen searched his expression for the reason he'd pulled away, but his eyes skipped over her face and focused on the TV.

Her lips felt cold, bereft, lonely. She wanted Nelson to sweep her into his arms and carry her to the bedroom, allow his caresses to chase away her worries and troubles. She'd gotten the impression by his kiss that he had wanted the same thing. "What's wrong?"

"Nothing," he asserted. Too loudly.

"Why did you stop?" He frowned. Would she ever learn to keep her mouth shut?

"Forget it, Ellen." He shoved a hand through his hair.

Okay, why the scowl, then? "But—"

"The timing isn't right," he argued.

"Is it because of my injury? You don't want to hurt me?" His silence sparked her anger. "Or maybe you've changed your mind about doing the down and dirty with a dairy farmer."

Brown eyes flashed.

Oh, Lord. She'd stepped out of bounds.

He pounced, forcing her head back on the pillow. His mouth tight. His nostrils flaring. Too bad his anger couldn't make the sweet yearning inside her go away. Tracing his jaw with her fingertips, she asked, "What is it, Nelson?" When he didn't answer, she added, "Tell me, because I really want to kiss you."

He rested his forehead against hers. "Hell, Ellen. I can't explain something I don't understand." He nuzzled his nose in her hair before trailing soft kisses down the side of her face and neck. His gaze, an odd mix of passion, regret and torment, bore into her. "I've dreamed about making love to you since the night we kissed on the swing."

Her heart sang.

"But…you're complicated."

Her heart hiccuped. "I've been called a lot of things in my life but never complicated."

"Maybe *complicated* is the wrong word." He brushed his lips against her forehead, then shifted away. "You married young and you don't have a lot of experience with relationships. You might get hurt."

Hurt? He'd already hurt her. "I get it. You believe that if we make love I'll expect an engagement ring." *And you don't have marriage in mind.*

When he avoided eye contact with her, she assumed she'd read him correctly. She sat up and shoved a finger under his nose. "Get this straight, Nelson. I may be nothing more than a farm girl, but I understand sex doesn't always lead to marriage or commitment. Did you ever consider I'm not ready for a serious relationship? Maybe I'd just like to have sex?" She hoped he wouldn't read the truth in her eyes—that yes, she did yearn for happily-ever-after. But only with the right man. Her heart argued Nelson was the right man. Her brain alleged the notion was ludicrous and if she was wise, she'd settle for sex and demand nothing more.

"What about Seth?"

"It's none of my son's business what happens between you and me." Regardless, the mood was spoiled. Forcing a change of topic, she inquired, "When did Seth get home?"

"He didn't. Brad's mother phoned earlier and asked if he could stay the night." He gestured to her leg. "Under the circumstances I didn't think you'd object."

No doubt Seth had blabbed about Nelson, and Brad's mother had jumped at the opportunity to do a little matchmaking. Arlene had never cared for Buck, and after he'd died, she'd told Ellen to set her sights higher next time. Nelson was higher. Way higher. "Who milked the cows?"

Nelson grinned—a boyish twist of the mouth that raised her blood pressure. "I did."

"You?" Visions of spilled milk and cows bolting from the barn with suction tubes attached to their udders flashed before her eyes.

"Piece of cake," he assured her. "Except for Betty. She wouldn't let me near to clean her sack."

"She hasn't been milked?"

"I made her wait until I milked the others. She liked me fine enough then."

"Betty always goes first."

He shrugged. "Next time, she'll cooperate."

"Aren't you a tough-love kind of man," she teased.

"You know it. Are you hungry?"

"For a vegetable casserole? No, thanks."

"How about a ham sandwich and a glass of milk?"

"You're sure the cows are okay?"

"I tucked every last one of them in for the night. Even sang them a lullaby."

"Yeah, sure." She swatted him playfully. He caught her hand and held it between his. "I guess I am hungry," she admitted.

He kissed her knuckles as if she were a real princess. "Be right back."

As soon as he left the room, she hauled herself off the couch, thankful he hadn't heard the foul word that flew out of her mouth. After wrapping the blanket around her waist, she limped to the bathroom. Using the toilet required a bit of maneuvering, but she managed with a minimal amount of discomfort. After washing up at the sink, she removed her dirty T-shirt and bra, tossed them into the clothes hamper, then slipped on the nightshirt hanging from the hook on the back of the door.

She hobbled to the living room, where Nelson was waiting to help her to the couch. They ate side by side in a comfortable silence until the *Tonight Show* ended. "Thank you for milking the cows, but you should have woken me. I could have—" His finger against her mouth stopped her protest.

"It's okay to let others help once in a while, Ellen."

"Like you ever let anyone take charge?"

He grinned. "I would if it was for the good of the company."

After a sizable stretch of silence, she said, "You think I'm an idiot for keeping the farm, don't you?"

"Not anymore."

Surprised, she asked, "What do you mean?"

"I'm learning this way of life has its advantages."

Advantages? He had to be kidding. "What advantages?"

"Feeling a sense of accomplishment after a hard day's work."

"And?"

"Handling a bunch of cows is a heck of a lot easier than dealing with people."

"Even Betty? She dug her little hooves in today and refused to be milked."

"True. But as far as employees go, Betty doesn't talk back and—" he grinned "—she doesn't beg for a raise."

"You act like milking cows is a great way to earn a living." If you could call her meager income a living.

Nelson turned thoughtful. "Each person has his own definition of success." Shrugging, he added, "I equate success with money."

That was a no-brainer.

"But there are people," he continued, "who don't

make a lot of money, yet are fulfilled and happy with their lives." He held her hand. She studied their entwined fingers, baffled by the strength, courage and comfort his grip offered.

"Are you happy, Ellen? Does the farm fulfill you?"

The question startled her. Did she dare lie and say yes? *No.* Nelson would see through her. "There have been times over the past thirteen years that I've felt fulfilled. Mostly before my parents died and there was extra help around the place." *When I had family who cared about me after Buck had lost interest.*

"Your husband's death must have been difficult."

Was Nelson a mind reader?

His fingers squeezed gently. "Living with your family and marrying so young…you've never really been on your own. Until now."

"I admit that when Buck died, I experienced a period of panic." Panic her husband had gone off and gotten himself killed and left her with debts she hadn't been aware of. Thank God his one credit card had had only a five-hundred-dollar balance.

"Do you plan to marry again?" he asked.

She flipped the question around on him. "Are you interested in marrying?" Not to her, of course, but to a rich, Chicago society girl.

"My career doesn't mix with a wife and family." He yanked her limp pigtail. "Promise me something."

"What?"

"Let me do the milking and the other chores until your leg heals."

The guy was nuts. "You expect me to sit on the

couch and watch talk shows all day while you create havoc in the barn?"

"Yes. Seth will help me."

The temptation to let him take the reins tugged at her something fierce. She might talk tough, but she recognized she was in no shape to lug fifty-pound milk cans around the barn. And if one of the cows became temperamental, she'd never be able to jump out of the way fast enough to avoid another kick.

Were it just her own welfare she had to worry about... But she had Seth to consider. If anything should happen to her, he'd end up in foster care. Buck's mother was still breathing, but she lived in a nursing home in Indiana, and his sister drove an eighteen-wheeler for a living. Not the life Ellen would choose for her son.

For God sakes, Ellen, don't be stupid. You're tired, hurt and you need rest. Let Nelson help. "Okay. I'll lay low for a couple of days, but I'm still working at the diner."

His smile, unabashedly male, was worth the blow to her pride. "I'll sleep on the couch tonight," he said.

"You can't—"

"I don't care for you being alone in the house," he stated.

Never bothered Buck one bit that she stayed by her lonesome when he worked construction. She decided it was nice to have someone worry about her—even if it was unnecessary.

Nelson got to his feet. "Time for bed."

Tired of being brave, tired of being alone, just plain tired...Ellen reached for Nelson's hand.

Chapter Nine

Nelson drove—rather, sped—through Four Corners, hoping Ellen wasn't staring out the window of Flo's Diner. If she spotted the car, she'd ring his cell phone and demand to know where he was headed and if Seth, whom he'd dropped off at Brad's house earlier, was with him.

He'd accompanied Seth to the front door of Brad's, and after the boys had shuffled down to the basement to play video games, he'd spoken with Brad's mother, Arlene. He'd volunteered to take the teens to tomorrow's Fourth of July celebration at the Klayton County Fair in Wayetteville.

Earlier in the morning, after Ellen had departed for the diner, Seth had appeared in the barn. Usually, the boy slept until noon, so Nelson assumed something had driven the kid out of bed. While helping with the milking, Seth had asked if Nelson had ever gone to a country fair. When he'd confessed he'd been to amusement parks and Disney World but never a fair, the teen had insisted Nelson was missing out on a great experience. Nelson doubted it, but didn't comment. Then Seth let slip—on purpose—that his mother had said they didn't have the money to go to the fair this year. As Seth had hoped, Nelson agreed to drive him and a friend.

Now, pressed for time, he drove ten miles over the speed limit. A week had passed since Ellen's injury and he was determined to stick his nose right where she said he could—in her business. He'd decided what to do, but in an uncharacteristic move, he dialed his brother's cell number on his BlackBerry. He'd never sought Ryan's counsel in the past and couldn't figure out why he was doing it now. "Hey, it's me."

"Nelson. Didn't plan to hear from you until the end of the summer. How do the overalls fit?" Ryan teased.

"Not funny. Listen, I need your advice." Silence. "Ryan, are you there?"

"I'm here. But shocked you're asking my opinion."

His brother's reaction didn't surprise him. Nelson considered seeking help a weakness, and had developed a habit of bluffing his way through problems he didn't have a clue how to resolve. Better to bluff than to appear a weak leader in front of his employees. Not that Ryan was his employee, but as the eldest brother, Nelson felt a deep sense of responsibility to be the one his brothers looked up to. "This has nothing to do with company business."

"Figures. What's the problem?"

"The problem is a *her.*"

A bark of laughter blasted through the connection and Nelson's eardrum protested. "You called the wrong guy. What do I know about women? My wife left me, remember?"

Ryan's former wife had been a rich debutante, big on charity work and shopping. But when it had come to real life, she hadn't had a backbone. His wife had displayed her true colors after his brother's close call with death during the 9/11 attack. Ryan hadn't even recovered from his injuries before she'd served him with divorce papers.

Nelson figured his brother was better off without the shallow bitch, but Ryan had yet to emerge from the corporate cave he'd holed himself up in since his divorce—six years ago. "It's not personal, Ryan. It's business."

Discussing Ellen was tempting. With his brother's aid he might understand exactly what it was he felt for the widow. He acknowledged his physical attraction to the pint-sized farmer, and he'd dated enough women in his lifetime to admit Ellen touched him on a deeper level. How deep was the million-dollar question. However, Ryan hadn't been romantically involved with a woman since his divorce, so Nelson intended to avoid the topic of male-female relationships. "Ellen Tanner is teetering on the edge of bankruptcy and she refuses to sell the farm."

"What about a bank loan?" Ryan suggested.

"She won't use the farm as collateral."

"Why don't you back her?"

In regard to business acumen, he and Ryan were well matched. Nelson had wrestled with the idea of investing in Ellen's farm. But each time he thought of her failing operation, he envisioned his investment dollars being fed into a shredder. "She won't accept my money."

"Pride?"

"Prideful, stubborn—"

"Sounds like Aaron's secretary, Martha," Ryan cut in.

"Convincing Ellen to accept money from me will be impossible."

"Then, big brother, convince the bank to accept something of yours as collateral."

"I could put up my new Jaguar. But how do I keep her from finding out?" Nelson pictured Ellen's face, dark with anger, when the bank manager explained the terms of the loan.

"Tell her she's signing insurance papers."

"That's underhanded."

"You have her best interests at heart, don't you?"

"Yes." Nelson believed he was helping Ellen because it was the right thing to do and not because he saw her situation as a business challenge he couldn't walk away from. *Are you sure about that?* Nelson was tempted to smash the conscience troll that had set up residence in his head the day he'd arrived at the Tanner farm.

"Any chance of a romantic development between you and this Ellen?" Ryan asked, interrupting Nelson's mental musings.

"She's a farmer."

"Jennifer's a construction foreman. If Aaron had had a problem with that, he wouldn't be marrying her."

"I'm not walking down any church aisle. Besides, Ellen has a son." Nelson believed Seth would jump at the chance to move to Chicago, but he was positive he wouldn't be around enough to be the kind of father the boy deserved. Or the kind of husband Ellen deserved. He devoted all his energy and time to the company. There was nothing left over for family.

But what if you could find time for a family....

"How old is the boy?"

Ryan's question broke Nelson's train of thought.

He wondered if his brother was remembering the child his ex-wife had aborted shortly after their divorce. "Seth is thirteen." Uncomfortable discussing Ellen and her son, he changed the subject. "How's Grandfather doing?"

"He's traveling to County Monaghan in Northern Ireland next week. Says he wants to visit Great-grandpa's village one more time."

"One more time? Is he ill?"

"He hasn't mentioned health problems."

"Go with him, Ryan. He shouldn't travel alone."

"He's not. He invited someone from Jennifer's neighborhood to accompany him."

"Who?"

"A woman named Mrs. Padrón. She's a widow, and Aaron says they've really hit it off."

A sign welcoming him to the nearby town of Bell sprang up alongside the road and Nelson slowed the car. "She's not after his money, is she?"

"Always the suspicious one, big brother. Aaron contends the old woman's intentions are honorable."

Nelson was shocked by his grandfather's interest in another woman. After his wife had died in the same plane crash that had killed Nelson's parents, his grandfather had never revealed a serious interest in another woman. "When is Grandfather due back in the country?"

"In time for Aaron's wedding in August."

Now he understood why his grandfather hadn't pestered him with phone calls the past few weeks. He'd been busy doing his own wooing.

"I've got another call beeping in, Nelson. I'd attempt a bank loan. Or convince her to sell to you, then rent the place back to her."

"Thanks for the advice, Ryan."

"As if you'll use any of it." His brother chuckled.

Before they hung up, Nelson felt compelled to ask, "Everything okay on your end?"

"Couldn't be better." Ryan's standard answer for the past few years. "Take care," he added, then disconnected the call.

When Nelson arrived in Bell, he decided to first secure the bank loan, then figure out how to convince Ellen to accept it.

"Hey, Ellen."

"Hi, Elmer. Have a seat. I'll be right with you." Ellen carried two lunch specials to a table near the front window. "Grilled cheese on sourdough, Mrs. Kasper." The elderly woman smiled her thanks. "And a meat loaf sandwich, burned around the edges, Mr. Kasper."

"Thank you, missy." The older man had gone to school with Ellen's father, but instead of farming, he'd attended college and had become a dentist. Semi-retired, he worked two days a week at a dental office in Bell. "How's Seth?" he asked.

"He's doing fine."

"If the boy's interested in earning extra cash this summer, my picket fence could use a new coat of paint. He can drop by anytime. Paint cans are in the barn."

The Kaspers lived in a beautiful, well-preserved 1910 Victorian home surrounded by several hundred acres of leased land. Last year, Seth had helped lay down new gravel in the driveway. Ellen suspected the older couple was aware she struggled to make ends meet. She hated accepting charity, but Seth had been thrilled when he'd used the income to purchase an expensive pair of sneakers he'd been wishing for for some time.

"I'll be sure to mention it to Seth." Ellen returned to the breakfast counter and set a fresh cup of coffee in front of Elmer. "The shop keeping you busy?"

The customer owned a car repair business five miles east of Four Corners. Divorced and in his mid fifties, with a touch of gray at the temples and a rock-solid gut, Elmer was a handsome man. For the past five years he'd eaten lunch at the diner twice a week in the hope of catching Flo's eye. But Flo had sworn off men, and Ellen figured Elmer was old enough to decide for himself if he could hold out another five years for Flo.

"Business is good," Elmer's eyes strayed to the kitchen door.

"I'll tell Flo you're out here."

"I'm not here to see Flo. I got news for you."

"Me?" *What kind of news?*

"It's about the feller you hired to work on your farm."

"Nelson? Why? What's wrong?"

"Don't get riled, gal. Your man was in Bell earlier this morning."

"He's not my man, Elmer. He's my employee."

"Your employee was at the bank."

"Which bank?" Bell had two.

"The credit union. I was making a withdrawal when I overheard him arguing with the loan manager."

Why would Nelson be arguing…unless…

"Didn't think much about it until your name was shouted across the bank lobby."

Unbelievable. Nelson had gone behind her back to secure a loan—money she didn't want. Would never be able to pay back. *Of all the nerve.* She spun on her rubber-soled shoes and stomped into the kitchen. "Flo, I'm taking a break."

"In the middle of lunch rush?"

"I have to run into Bell—"

"Bell's forty minutes away."

Not the way I plan to drive. "Nelson's stirring up trouble. I'll be back as soon as I can." She paused at the door and removed her apron. "Elmer's here. He said he'd help." She tossed the apron at Elmer. "Flo would appreciate you covering for me." If she wasn't so ticked at Nelson, she might have laughed at the way the car mechanic's mouth flapped wordlessly.

No telling how much damage Nelson had done, she

thought as she pulled into the credit union a short time later. She was astonished Nelson's fancy black sports car remained parked in the lot. If he'd spent this long in the bank, then he had to be scheming more than a loan. Probably a second mortgage on the farm. Forcing herself to remain calm, she parked the truck, then entered the building.

Two bank tellers were helping customers at the counter, and the help desk sat empty. Could Nelson have left his car in the lot while he had lunch across the street at Simon's Deli? Before she made up her mind to stay or go, a voice drifted out of an office at the far end of the lobby. Curious, she crossed the floor and eavesdropped outside the open door.

The name etched into the frosted glass read Milton Montrose, Loan Manager. Good ol' Milt. Ellen had never cared for the man—a high-school classmate of hers. Milton had attended college, then returned to Bell and worked for the credit union ever since.

"Ellen Tanner is a bad risk, Mr. McKade. I don't know how many other ways I can get that across to you." Milton's voice vibrated with frustration.

"If you believe Ellen's a bad risk, then you're not familiar with her at all. She's ethical, upstanding and dependable. I'm confident that if I co-sign the loan, she'll pay back the money," Nelson persisted.

Co-sign a loan? *No way.* She battled the urge to burst into the office and give both men a piece of her mind and her fist. But something held her back. Maybe it was the possessive note in Nelson's voice when he'd defended her. She'd always fought her own battles—preferred it that way. So why did she all of a sudden feel so alone? If she wasn't careful, she could become used to Nelson watching her back. But then when he left at the end of the summer, she'd feel betrayed.

"I don't understand why you care about the Tanner farm. The place has been mismanaged for years. If she'd listened to her husband when he'd been alive and sold the farm when property values around here were worth something, she wouldn't be in this predicament."

"The farm is Ellen's home. Where she desires to raise her son. Reason enough to grant her a loan."

"The bank doesn't agree. I have better things to do, Mr. McKade, than argue over a loan that's not going to materialize."

A moment later, Nelson stormed out of the office, unaware Ellen hovered behind the door. Before she had a chance to follow, Milton spotted her. His lip curled. "Spying, Ellen?"

"You're an ass, Milton," she spat, then hurried off after Nelson. Once outside the bank, she called his name.

He stopped. When she caught up to him, he grumbled, "Aren't you supposed to be at the diner?"

"Elmer spilled the beans."

"Who's Elmer?"

"He owns the Fender-Bender Auto Repair. What made you believe I'd allow you to co-sign a bank loan for me?" She rolled up on her tiptoes, adding another inch to her short height.

"You have apple pie in your hair." His eyes twinkled.

"What?"

"Here." He tugged a strand of hair from her pony-tail, then held the glob of pie filling in front of her nose.

"Oh, for crying out loud." She slapped his hand, sending the pie crumb sailing through the air. "You're distracting me."

His face sobered. "How much did you hear?"

"Enough to understand you're sticking your nose where it doesn't belong."

"You *told* me I could help you."

"Have you been drinking?" She leaned forward and sniffed his mouth—minty. He'd probably chewed a stick of gum before entering the bank.

"No, but I could sure as hell use a drink now." He rubbed his forehead. "The reason I tried to secure a loan is that you gave me permission to help you."

"When?"

"The day Bones kicked you in the leg."

Ellen's mind raced as she struggled to recall their conversation. She'd been exhausted and injured—who knows what she'd blabbed.

"You agreed I could take over."

"I assumed you were referring to milking the cows for a few days while my leg healed. I didn't realize you intended to run my life."

His eyes flashed with what...hurt? She felt bad she had yelled at him. "Whatever I said, I didn't mean. Even if you could talk Milton into loaning me money, I wouldn't accept a cent from him. During high school I refused to date him, so when I ended up pregnant, he spread rumors that I'd intended to trap Buck into marriage. The guy's a jerk."

"I'm sorry."

"Stop interfering, Nelson. I hired you to watch Seth and do a few chores. You were supposed to make my life easier, not more difficult."

"What you don't understand, Ellen, is that something has to give or you'll lose the farm."

The hard note in his voice convinced her she could no longer ignore her problems and hope a miracle dropped from the sky and solved her cash-flow troubles. A sob clogged her throat, making it painful to swallow. "How much *giving* do I have to do?"

Nelson must have noticed her distress, because he cupped her cheek and rubbed the pad of his thumb back and forth across her skin in a comforting rhythm. "I'm not positive, but I promise I'll find a way for you to keep the farm."

She yearned to believe him. Desperately ached to believe. "I have to return to the diner before Flo fires me." She stepped sideways, then paused. "Where's Seth?" In all the excitement she'd forgotten her son wasn't with Nelson.

"I dropped him off at Brad's house. He's staying the night, then I'm treating the boys to the county fair tomorrow. I was hoping you'd come along."

Her son must have mentioned she didn't have the money to go this year. Her first instinct was to decline, but it had been forever since she'd spent a day having fun with Seth. His happiness was worth more than her pride. "I'd love to tag along."

"Good. I'll pick up a pizza for dinner. Drive carefully."

Pizza, Nelson and no Seth. The possibilities were endless.

"SUPPER'S ALMOST READY." Ellen's announcement greeted Nelson as he walked through the front door, carrying a clean set of clothes and his shaving kit. He slipped off his work boots and set them on the rug. When he glanced up, Ellen stood in the kitchen doorway, wiping her hands on a towel. Something inside his chest caught at the delicate smile curving her lips.

He was thirty-seven years old. Most men his age were married. For a moment, he envisioned entering his apartment and finding Ellen waiting. The notion shook him. He admitted he was a miserable failure at juggling a career and a relationship. He might believe Ellen was the one woman who could cure him of his 24-7 work ethic. But not for long. Deep in his gut, he believed his drive to succeed would demand he stay longer at the office, work weekends and travel on business trips more often. It wouldn't be fair to Ellen or Seth. But a guy could dream....

"Do you mind if I take a shower first?" he asked.

She'd already showered. Tendrils of damp hair curled around her face and the remaining strands were pinned to the top of her head with a big clip. He mentally chastised himself for thinking he could smell her fruit-scented shampoo over the spicy smells of the pizza warming in the oven.

"If you make it quick," she murmured.

Her words barely registered. His attention was glued to her pale lavender tank top, which accentuated the perfect roundness of her small breasts. His gaze roamed lower, checking out her frayed denim cutoffs. Her legs were gorgeous—toned and firm. The bruising on her thigh had faded to a yellow-green and was barely noticeable.

A sudden gust of heat slapped his body, and it wasn't from the hot wind blowing through the living room window but from the realization that Seth was spending the night at his friend's, leaving him and Ellen alone in the house.

"I'll hurry," he mumbled, then forced his gaze from her sexy little body and hustled down the hallway. After he entered the bathroom, he locked the door, not sure if he intended to keep himself locked in or Ellen locked out. He showered and shaved in record time, put on a pair of khaki shorts and a golf shirt, then slipped on his sandals and returned to the kitchen just as Ellen carried a load of his clean laundry in from the back porch.

"You didn't have to wash my clothes." He reached for the pile. "But I appreciate it just the same."

"You've been here over a month and you haven't used the washing machine. Exactly how many pairs of underwear do you own?"

Ellen ought to know if she rummaged through the two large duffel bags of dirty laundry he stored in his room in the barn. "I stocked up before I left Chicago."

"In the pantry you'll find the bottle of red wine someone sent me for Christmas." She pulled the pizza from the oven.

He placed the clothes on the living-room couch, then searched the pantry. He hadn't had a glass of good wine since he'd arrived at the farm. According to the label on the bottle, he'd have to wait until he went back to Chicago to have one.

In a matter of minutes, Ellen had the table set, the pizza cut and a salad ready. He filled the wineglasses, then held out a chair for Ellen.

Her gaze avoided his face when she thanked him. Was Ellen contemplating the same thing—that they were alone tonight? They ate in silence for a few minutes, their eyes occasionally meeting, then skirting away.

"I can't stand this." Ellen tossed her napkin on the table, shoved her chair back and stood. Face flushed, she wrung her hands, shifting from one foot to the other.

Careful to maintain a neutral expression, he asked, "Can't stand what?"

"This—" she flung her hand through the air "—whatever is happening between us."

He knew exactly the whatever Ellen referred to—the subtle brushes against one another when they milked the cows together. The hungry stares she sent his way when she assumed he wasn't aware. The heated glances he shot right back at her when she wasn't paying attention.

He set his fork on the plate and left his chair. Her eyes widened a fraction as he drew near. When mere inches separated them, he lowered his head and whispered, "You mean this whatever?" He brushed his mouth across hers. Slowly. Thoroughly.

"Mmm."

"Are we on the same page, here?" He captured her lips in another searing kiss.

"I think so," she murmured against his mouth.

As if someone had thrown a cooler of cold Gatorade over his head, the word think stopped him cold. "You're not sure?"

"It's been a long time. I...I..."

He pressed a finger to her mouth. "It's been a while for me, too."

"Nelson, I'm not like those city women you've... you've..."

"You better not be." He slipped the clip from her hair and spread the damp strands across her shoulder. "So...?"

"So...?" She smiled.

"Will you let this city boy make out with you in the hayloft?"

Chapter Ten

"You're not serious, are you?" Ellen asked, sure Nelson was joking. No one with an ounce of sense would make love on dusty, insect-ridden, scratchy hay.

"Don't farm girls prefer the barn to a bed?" Grinning, Nelson smoothed a strand of hair behind her ear, and she shivered at the casual caress.

Maybe it was her imagination, but since Bones had kicked her in the leg, it sure seemed that Nelson *touched* her more often. Little touches—grabbing her elbow to steady her. Clasping her hand for no good reason she could figure out. Setting his palm against her lower back as he held the door open for her. Playfully yanking her ponytail.

She didn't want their first time to be in the hayloft. The prospect of making love with Nelson, a man she was positive had a lot more experience than she did with the act, was daunting enough on clean cotton sheets. Her palms itched—a sign of nerves. *Maybe the timing is off.*

Are you crazy? Shut down your analytical brain,

Ellen. Nelson—gorgeous, nice, considerate, bossy, demanding, pushy Nelson—is right here in front of you, ready and willing to ensure your wildest dreams come true.

His mouth inched nearer. "Second thoughts?"

At least a thousand. "None." His kisses were the stuff of fantasies, the right amount of pressure and tongue to tantalize, tease and excite.

An image of Buck swept through her mind, but she blocked it out, refusing to feel any guilt that she enjoyed Nelson's kisses more. *Nelson will give you a night to remember. A memory to replay during the long, cold winter when you lie alone in bed.* A memory was more than Buck had ever given her.

Be careful, Ellen. Memories are good, but Nelson has the power to destroy your heart. A power Buck had never possessed in all the years they'd been married. She rested her hand against Nelson's chest, and immediately he broke the kiss, concern darkening his brown eyes.

He cupped her face. "Don't be afraid, Ellen. I promise you this isn't a one-night stand." He nuzzled her forehead. "You're unlike any woman I've ever met. One moment you frustrate the hell out of me—the next you make me laugh."

"You sure know how to woo a gal."

"Other women have made me smile here." He touched her finger to a corner of his mouth. "But you're the first woman who's ever made me smile here," he assured her, dragging her hand to his heart.

"Well, now. Those are better wooing words." Ellen

swore her heart pounded in rhythm with Nelson's, which was banging beneath her palm.

"I can't promise. My job is in Chicago and—" he swallowed hard "—yours is here."

She caressed his clean-shaven jaw. "I understand, but—"

"You don't want to get hurt," he finished, then hugged her.

She wondered at the probability of Nelson falling in love with her. Could a man like him find something in her to love? Something worth taking a chance on? She nestled her head under his chin.

"The one thing I'm sure about, Ellen, is my desire to make love to you. To hold you in my arms…feel your skin against mine…kiss you all over."

Quit analyzing.

Stop second-guessing.

Just feel.

There will never be another Nelson. Grab what he's offering—real, honest-to-goodness passion between a man and woman. Wallow in it. Soak up every last drop of ecstasy. Then, when it's time, send him off with a wave and a smile.

She wiggled from his grasp, clasped his hand and led the way to her bedroom. "Trust me, you'd rather have a mattress under you than hay."

"Speaking from experience…?"

"Maybe," Ellen teased.

He grinned. "Okay. No hayloft. But I'm picking the next place."

A tiny thrill raced through her at the notion that

he intended to make love to her again. And maybe again. Edgy, she tugged her hand free and padded across the room to the bed. He stayed in the doorway, a shoulder propped against the frame, his gaze riveted on the bed. Not her.

Understanding dawned. "I never slept with Buck in here."

He shuddered at her pronouncement. Nelson amazed her. That it would bother him to love her on the same bed another man had slept in caused her heart to flip crazily. "This was my parents' room. After they died, Seth moved in here. He was so excited he didn't have to sleep on the couch anymore." She smiled at the memory. "When Buck died, Seth and I switched rooms." *Then I was the excited one…giving up the bed, along with the memories of sleeping with her husband.*

Nelson's solemn brown-eyed stare unnerved Ellen. Had she said too much? Wrecked the mood? After a long pause he cleared his throat. "You've lived a very different life than I have."

She didn't want his pity. Her life hadn't been all bad. "We had some fun times packed in this house like sardines." The comment caused him to smile.

He lifted a hand. Beckoned her. He could ask almost anything and she'd comply. She shuffled across the floor and threaded her fingers through his.

"I'm glad you are who you are, Ellen Tanner." His serious expression tempted her to believe their fairy-tale evening would evolve into forever. But she acknowledged it wouldn't.

Then he kissed her. As far as kisses went, Nelson's were to die for. The room spun. Tilted. Wavered until she was forced to shut her eyes and clasp his shoulders to keep from tumbling to the floor.

So this is what it feels like to be desired. Coveted. Maybe even loved a little.

Something inside her shifted. Broke loose. A hunger. A yearning to shut the door on reality. A desire to put herself first and *take, take, take* until she felt sated, fat with happiness—even if the happiness expired with tomorrow's sunrise.

Farmers didn't fantasize. Ellen was a realist and understood that her relationship with Nelson had nowhere to go but across the room to the bed. So be it. She deserved a taste of heaven. A moment of brilliance in her otherwise dull existence.

Her breath left her lungs in a loud swoosh when he swooped her up into his arms and deposited her on the mattress. His gaze never leaving her face, he removed his shirt, then his shorts and sandals. Tonight he wore silk boxers. Red. She caressed the hem of the leg opening. Slipped her fingertip under the material and stroked his thigh.

Growling, he sprawled atop her, his feet dangling over the edge of the bed. "I dream about you."

The air around her thickened. She labored to catch her breath. "You do?"

"At night, I close my eyes and the scent of you fills my head." He held her hand in front of his face and studied the calluses and short, blunt nails. "I fantasize about what these hardworking hands would feel like against my skin." He held her fingers to his bare chest and groaned.

Surprised her less-than-beautiful hands brought him pleasure, she traced the ridges and planes of his torso. Scraped her nails through the light dusting of hair across his pectoral muscles. When she trailed a finger down his stomach to the waistband of his boxers, he sucked in a quick breath, then lowered his head and kissed her.

A man of many talents, he'd worked her clothes off and his boxers with their mouths still fused. Left in nothing but her birthday suit, she lay vulnerable and exposed to his admiring gaze.

She wasn't ashamed of her body. After all, she was a farmer and exercise was part of her everyday existence. Her muscles were toned and firm and she didn't carry an ounce of extra fat anywhere. But she wasn't perfect. Seth had been a large baby and the pregnancy had left her belly covered in silver scars. Automatically, she tried to hide them, but Nelson captured her wrist.

"Don't, Ellen. You're a beautiful woman and a wonderful mother." He traced one of the feathery lines with his fingertip, leaving a path of fire in its wake. "Seth is lucky to have you."

Shoving her hands into his thick, unruly hair, she tugged his head closer. "Let's not discuss Seth." This time *she* kissed *him*.

Swept up in a vortex of vivid color and sensation, she gave herself over to Nelson's expertise. He held her, caressed her, cherished her as if her body were a temple to be worshiped. His mouth was everywhere—her neck, her shoulder, her belly and oh…! He smothered her, devoured her, relished her.

"Ellen." Someone called her name. "Ellen." She ignored it, instead focusing on the incredible sensation of heat escalating through her body. "Ellen." Annoyed, she opened her eyes and frowned at Nelson's face, hovering above hers.

"Do we need protection?"

When his question finally sank in, she blushed. "I went off the pill over a year ago."

"Not to worry." He leaned across her body, flattening her breasts with his chest, and snagged his shorts off the floor. After rummaging through a pocket, he removed a foil package and held it in the air like a victory trophy.

Smoothing a hand down his bare buttocks, she purred, "Do you always carry a condom in your pocket?"

"Only when I'm feeling lucky." He thrust his erection against her stomach.

"How often do you feel lucky?" She meant it as a joke but she hoped he didn't do one-night stands often.

His eyes softened. "I haven't felt lucky in a long, long time."

"I'm glad." She sighed into his neck, curled her feet over his calves and raised her breasts, silently begging. His mouth settled over a nipple, drawing an unladylike moan from her. There was something deeply intimate about a man's mouth on a woman's breast.

Nelson was a master at playing her body, at wringing responses she was sure would mortify her in the morning when her brain cleared and she could think again.

Arms and legs tangled, forming a slippery knot upon the sheets. She and Nelson shifted position from top to bottom to side and back to top. She would never have guessed in-control-of-everything Nelson was such an out-of-control and enthusiastic lover. "No more…" she whined after her second trip to the stars.

"One more time, angel." His kiss—tender and sweet—made her almost believe she was an angel.

He captured her mouth, his tongue sweeping inside. He cupped her breast, cherished the small mound with his mouth, drawing an embarrassing whimper from her, followed by a lusty sigh when he suckled her nipple.

She struggled to keep pace on the maddening journey. Then his hand delved between her thighs, weakening her resolve. Hovering somewhere between consciousness and unconsciousness, she begged for mercy. Her prayers were answered when Nelson drove into her and released her from the prison of passion he'd held her in.

His thrusts quickened, increasing the intensity of the tremors pulsing through her body and shooting her into the heavens. Moments later, his groan vaguely registered in the back of her mind.

Shadows danced in the corners of the bedroom when Ellen awoke. How long had she been asleep? Nelson's hair scratched her nose and quiet snores escaped his mouth. In sleep, he had wrapped an arm around her middle and had rested his face against her breasts. She felt safe and secure. *And loved.* For this one night.

Buck had never cuddled with her after sex. Nope. He'd popped off the bed, showered, grabbed a beer and then watched TV until all hours of the morning.

And he never called you angel.

A warm gush flooded her heart. Secretly, she was fiercely glad Nelson's grandfather had answered her newspaper ad. The memory of Nelson's lovemaking would last forever.

Tears blurred her vision, but she refused to cry. Tomorrow, she'd wake up and be a farmer again. Tonight, she was Cinderella and Nelson was her Prince Charming.

SOMETHING TICKLED Nelson's thigh. He ignored the irritation, instead concentrating on the soft plumpness beneath his cheek. He skimmed his palm across smooth satin skin—*Ellen.*

He fought to remain in the lethargic state of semi sleep, where he could fantasize about the woman in his arms and snuggle against her feminine form. But the damn tickle refused to go away. He swatted the air above his thigh.

The *plumpness* jiggled.

Little tease. He brushed his hand over his leg a second time. The tickle moved to the patch of skin below his left ear. How long did Fanny Farmer intend to toy with him?

He shifted, feigning sleep, and skimmed his mouth over her nipple. Her body stiffened, then relaxed when he nestled his face in her cleavage.

The one thing he'd learned about Ellen during their endless hours of bodily exploration was that she loved having her breasts caressed and kissed. Good thing, since he loved lavishing attention on them. Small, round and enough to fill his hands, with a bit left over. Perfect.

Nelson cracked an eyelid and checked the clock radio on the nightstand. 2:00 a.m. They'd made love twice before Ellen had fallen into a contented sleep. But he'd lain awake and stared at the ceiling light fixture, troubled by the edge of desperation he'd sensed in her lovemaking—as if she'd feared this would be the last time in her life she'd become intimate with a man…with *him*.

From their first kiss to their first touch, he'd been aware of her lack of sexual experience. That hadn't bothered him. What had worried him most was the idea her husband had never cherished her. How could a man *not* treasure a woman like Ellen? Sure, she was willful, stubborn and flat-out wrong about a lot of things, but he'd never met a female more determined. So passionate about her beliefs.

Ellen's independence bowled him over. She was by far the strongest woman he'd ever encountered. He might not agree with her reasons to keep the farm, but she had a right to choose to live her life the way she saw fit. His mind understood. But his heart ached when he realized her choices might cause her to go through life alone. With no protector. No man to guard her back. Or to offer a shoulder to rest her weary head on.

After making love, he'd held Ellen in his arms and had imagined himself her knight in shining armor— the man to whisk her away from a future of nothing but endless work, difficult times and debt.

Marriage.

Marriage had never been in his plans. Running Mc-Kade Import-Export was more than a full-time job. He considered the hours and energy he expended in order to keep tabs on all three offices. Would his work ethic change if he were married to Ellen? Would he delegate some of his responsibilities to his brothers and staff in order to devote more time to a wife and children?

Was he willing to loosen his iron-clad grip on the company in exchange for a family—Ellen and Seth. If so, was the promise of a future with Nelson enough to entice Ellen away from the farm?

She would if you loved her.

Who said anything about love? He cared for Ellen. Hell, yes, he cared. *But love?*

His internal struggle must have registered with her because the tickle stopped. "Nelson, you okay?" she murmured.

Rising up on an elbow, he winked. "More than okay. You?"

One delicate shoulder lifted as her gaze slid from his face.

Did she regret their intimacy? "What's wrong?"

Her mouth formed a sexy pout, then she sighed. "Just bored."

Bored? Caught off guard by her playfulness, he grinned. "I have a cure for boredom."

"You do?" She flung her arms around his neck, then murmured against his mouth, "Show me."

The sweet smell of her skin mixed with the heady aroma of their lovemaking wrapped him in a sensual haze. Her lips conformed to his, igniting sparks inside him. He must be losing his mind—their third time making love and each caress, each kiss, felt and tasted brand-new.

He trailed his mouth down her neck, skimmed over her breasts and across her flat tummy, working his way to the blond vee between her thighs. The first time, he'd had to coax her to open for him, but now she lifted her hips off the mattress. Eager. Greedy.

He intended to savor her body—her scent, the slickness of her moist skin, the sound of her sighs. Ellen had other plans.

Her hands moved over his muscles in aggressive, sweeping caresses, the tips of her nails leaving a red mark in their wake. She wrapped her legs around his waist and bumped her pelvis against his stomach.

So much for slow and easy.

Ellen's eagerness challenged his urge to control as he strained to keep pace with her frantic movements. He attempted to calm her with a tender kiss, but she'd have none of it. First she bit his lip, then she sucked his tongue into her mouth. He'd barely gotten the condom on, before she uttered an obscene command in his ear.

He lost it.

Surging inside her, he thrust, stroke after stroke. He loved her with rawness. Demand. Power. In seconds, Ellen's body stiffened and her guttural cry brought about his release.

Summoning what was left of his strength, he rolled off her. Side by side, they stared at each other, chests heaving, sweat trickling off their bodies.

"What the hell just happened, Ellen?"

Her eyes twinkled. "I'm not sure, but that was fun."

Fun? His head had almost exploded and she thought the past 120 seconds of crazy had been fun?

"It's never been like that for me." She threaded her fingers through his.

"Me, neither." The way he'd lost himself in her sweet loving terrified him. "Ellen Tanner, you are the most fascinating woman I have ever had the pleasure of knowing."

This time she let him take the lead, and he made darn sure to amply reward her team spirit.

Chapter Eleven

"Wait until you see Deep Throat." Seth spoke from the back seat.

In the process of parking the sports car in the gravel lot outside the Klayton County fairgrounds, Nelson jabbed his foot against the brake, causing Ellen to clutch the dashboard. She nibbled her lower lip to keep from laughing at his stunned expression. Did he honestly believe she'd allow her son to view porn movies?

Nelson shut off the engine. "What kind of fair brings in actors and actresses like that?"

"Deep Throat's not an actor—he's a sword swallower," Seth explained.

"Cutlery and an occasional butcher knife," Ellen clarified, grinning at Nelson's misassumption.

By all rights, Ellen should be exhausted, not invigorated, excited and energetic. If someone had predicted she'd feel this perky after a night of incredible sex, where her partner had thoroughly explored, experimented and tested the limits of her body until exhaustion had overtaken her, she would have sworn the person had lost his or her marbles.

But that was exactly what Nelson had done—
ravished her.

Over and over. Until the wee morning hours when
they'd collapsed into sated unconsciousness, only to
be jarred awake by the clock-radio alarm.

She'd rolled her tender, still tingly body off the
bed and had stumbled to the barn. Nelson had joined
her several minutes later. Between passionate kisses,
lewd caresses and a breath-stealing quickie up against
the barn door, they'd managed to milk the cows. She
should have expected he would be as demanding a
lover as he was with everything he laid his hands on.

"Are you coming?" Nelson asked.

Coming? Heat suffused her face and she prayed the
young backseat passengers hadn't noticed. *Fat chance.*

"Mom, why's your face all red?"

"Your mom needs fresh air. Everybody out." Nelson's
eyes sparkled. "Shame on you, Widow Tanner."

"Me? What for?"

Leaning over the gearshift, he taunted, "For every
single sexy thought running through your mind right
now."

She couldn't very well confess making love with
Nelson had revealed a sensual side of herself she
hadn't known existed. Nelson was like candy. One
taste and all she could do was dream of when she
could have another piece. *Of him.* Before she got herself into a heap of trouble, she planted a quick kiss on
his cheek and scooted from the car.

"Are you sure we can't stay for the Midget Men
Monster Truck Jam tonight, Mom?" Seth whined.

The Klayton County Fair Board had a reputation for booking outrageous entertainment events such as tonight's—little people driving five-ton megatrucks with 66-inch tires. The event didn't hold much appeal to her, but she could understand where the boys might enjoy the ruckus. "I'm sorry, Seth. The cows have to be milked by six."

"Maybe my dad could pick us up afterward," Brad offered.

No way was she leaving two thirteen-year-olds alone at an event where beer and who-knows-what-else flowed freely in the stands. "Sorry, guys." Time to change the subject. "There's the ticket-booth line." She pointed up ahead.

"Race you," Brad challenged. The boys took off down the runway, dodging bodies, strollers and a ferret on a leash.

"I could milk the cows, then return for all of you tonight," Nelson said.

"That's generous of you, but I guarantee that by late afternoon, the boys will be more than ready to leave." As she and Nelson followed at a slower pace, Ellen asked, "Have you ever been to a fair?"

"Disney World, Six Flags amusement parks, but never anything smaller." His mouth dropped open when a wheelchair-bound granny wearing a skimpy halter top and a miniskirt winked at him.

Swallowing her laughter, Ellen insisted, "You're in for a real treat." And she wasn't referring to the sunny, slightly breezy eighty-degree weather.

"Do you attend the fair every year?" Nelson side-stepped to avoid squishing a half-eaten, mustard-covered corn dog.

"Try to. My parents could never afford real vacations, so a trip to the country fair was my sole summer entertainment. I got involved in 4-H when I was in middle school and for a couple of years I showed dairy cattle."

"Win any ribbons?" He swatted at a pesky fly buzzing around his head.

"No. I mostly did it because I enjoyed hanging out with the other farm kids in the livestock barns."

Nelson smacked his brow with his open hand.

"Here." She held out a tissue.

"What's that for?"

"You have a dead fly stuck to your forehead."

"Oh, hell." He spat on the tissue, then wiped off the gooey remains of the insect.

Seth waved from his place in line as they approached. Before she'd even unzipped her fanny pack, Nelson insisted, "I'm paying." He opened his wallet and handed each boy a twenty. "That should hold you for a little while."

"Gee, thanks, Mr. McKade." Seth grinned.

"Yeah, thanks, Mr. McKade," Brad added. "We're going on the Tilt-A-Whirl first."

A college-aged guy strolled past and whistled. Ellen smiled, then schooled her expression when she noticed Nelson frowning at her.

"That happen often?" he muttered.

"Yeah. Guys are always looking at Mom," Seth volunteered.

Nelson examined her pink cotton tank top, frayed-at-the-edges denim shorts and white sneakers. "You don't say."

"Good thing she's hanging around you, Mr. Mc-Kade. Guys won't hit on her now."

"Enough already. We'll catch up with you boys later." Ellen led Nelson toward a row of tents off the main runway.

"Shouldn't we arrange a meeting place?" he asked.

"As soon as the boys blow through their money, they'll track us down."

"But—"

Ellen appreciated Nelson's worrying over Seth and his friend. "They'll be fine," she reassured him.

"What if they get hungry? Maybe I should give them some more money."

"No. I'd rather they run out of cash and have to find us than not see them all day."

Nelson's face lit with understanding, then just as quickly, he frowned. "Who the heck is he?"

Ellen followed his gaze to a tent several yards away. "Tattoo Man." She waved at the carnival worker, who sat on an ancient pickle barrel. The carnival worker raised a hand and flashed a tobacco-stained grin.

"You know the guy?" No mistaking the shock in Nelson's voice.

"I first met Tattoo Man when I was in fifth grade. Oh, boy, did I have a crush on him." When Nelson's eyebrows rose several inches, she added, "He had all his teeth back then."

Nostalgia tweaked Ellen's heart as they drew near the aging man. She could no longer make out the pirate ship tattooed on his stomach. She remembered the first time she'd watched him wiggle his abdominal muscles. The ship moved as if it sailed on water. Now only the mast remained visible; the rest was lost in the rolls of sagging skin and belly flab.

"C'mon, I'll introduce you." She ignored Nelson's sputter as they stopped in front of the purple-and-gold tent. "Hello, Mr. Tattoo Man. This is my friend Nelson McKade. He's working on the farm this summer."

Nelson held out his hand. "Pleasure to meet you, sir."

The respect Nelson showed the old man tugged at Ellen's heart. She was positive he had never in his life associated with a person like Tattoo Man, yet he treated the man with dignity—something she suspected the carnival employee had not experienced often in his illustrious career.

Tattoo Man shot tobacco out of the gap between his front teeth, then grabbed Ellen's hand and held it tenderly between his wrinkled, arthritic fingers. "Missed you last year, missy." He motioned with his head to the game booth across the runway. "Lola told me about your husband."

Ellen waved at the woman manning the duck shootin' booth. Lola had gone through school with Ellen but had dropped out in tenth grade to run off with a ride operator from the fair. Happily married to the same man, and mother of four children, Lola—and her family—traveled throughout the year with various carnival companies.

"Seth and I are doing fine," she assured Tattoo Man.

"You ready to marry me and join the carnival now?" A sparkle shone through his cloudy eyes.

"I'm still considering…."

"Fickle woman."

"Maybe I'll have an answer for you next summer."

"Been sayin' that for nigh on twenty years."

"You might have to wait another twenty." She smiled.

"Don't reckon you'll ever let me rest in peace."

"Not on your life." She kissed his whiskered cheek. Face glowing red, he reached for his pack of Camels. "Tell that boy of yers to stop by. I got a new tattoo to show him."

"Will do."

He waved. "Go on now. You and yer feller have a good time."

With a parting smile, she clasped Nelson's hand and they walked off. Every other step his fingers tightened around hers, then relaxed. "Something on your mind?" she asked.

"You didn't…I mean you two were never…that is—"

Startled, she stumbled and Nelson grabbed her elbow. Never would she have suspected that such a confident, self-assured man would be jealous of a toothless old scalawag.

Nelson's eyes skidded away from hers. "I didn't think so," he muttered.

She rewarded him with a hug before they continued walking. "Tattoo Man was like a stepfather to me. A few times over the years I spilled my guts to him. He'd listen to my dreams and never once say they were silly or senseless." Her voice dropped. "And the summer I showed up with Seth in a baby buggy all he said was, 'With you for a mama, he'll grow up to be a fine young man.'"

"I'm glad he was there for you." They strolled for over an hour, stopping to play several games. Nelson was determined to win her a stuffed animal, but after spending twenty-five dollars and coming up empty-handed, she begged, "No more."

"I'm sure I can knock over those milk bottles," he boasted, ignoring her protest. He laid five dollars on the edge of the booth, picked up the baseball, wound his arm like a Major League baseball pitcher, then—to Ellen's amazement—knocked over every bottle on the first try.

"Yeah!" She flung her arms around his neck and planted a big smooch on his lips.

"Which one, lady?" The booth operator held up three prizes.

"The pink cow, please." When Nelson handed her the toy—the size of a Kleenex box—she hugged it to her chest. "No one's ever won me a stuffed animal before."

"Good." He checked his watch. "Should we find the boys and grab a bite to eat?"

"A hot dog sounds good." Hand in hand, they wove through the growing crowd of fairgoers.

"Mom! Mom!"

Ellen spun at the sound of Seth's voice and spotted the boys in line for the bumper cars. "There they are." She squeezed Nelson's hand.

"What's that?" Seth pointed to the pink cow.

"Nelson won me this."

"Kinda dinky, ain't it?" Seth elbowed Brad and the two boys giggled.

Nelson's wounded expression made it almost impossible to refrain from joining in the laughter, but she managed to keep a straight face. "Hungry?" she asked.

Seth and Brad stared longingly at the bumper cars.

Nelson must have understood the boys didn't want to give up their place in line, because he slipped another couple of twenties from his wallet and handed them over. "Grab a hot dog after the ride."

"Sweet," the teens echoed in unison, exchanging a conspiring grin.

"Don't spend it all on rides or games. Make sure to eat something so you don't get sick."

"Yes, Mom."

"Sure, Mrs. Tanner."

She and Nelson ambled off to a chorus of "Thank you, Mr. McKade."

"I have money, Nelson. I wish you'd stop paying for everything." She hated to admit she had only fifty dollars in her fanny pack. But she also didn't want Nelson believing she was a moocher.

"Okay. You can buy my hot dog. What smells so good around here?" He sniffed the air.

"Fried onion rings." She nodded to a vendor.

They stopped at the small white hut, ordered onion rings and hot dogs, then devoured them standing because there were no empty tables. When they had finished, Ellen asked, "Ready to meet another friend of mine?"

"Does this one have body piercings?"

"No. But Tizzy has the world's longest neck."

Nelson's eyes narrowed. "You're not kidding, are you?"

"C'mon. She's a really sweet lady and famous, too. She traveled with Ringling Brothers, Barnum and Bailey circus for several years."

"What's her story?" he asked, following her across the grounds to a second grouping of colorful tents.

"She was born in a village along the Thai-Burma border near India. Her mother came from the Pai Dong Long Neck People. Tizzy got her first neck ring when she turned six."

"That young? Will her neck break if she removes the rings?"

"No. The neck doesn't really stretch. Over time, the heavy brass rings crushed her collarbones, creating an illusion of a longer neck."

"How did she end up in America traveling with a carnival?"

"I asked her once, but she didn't go into detail. She would only say she'd been banned from her tribe at the age of fifteen. She joined a circus in India, and when they traveled to America, someone from Ringling Brothers offered her a job, so she stayed in the United States."

They rounded a corner, then Ellen stopped suddenly in front of the red tent.

"What's wrong?" Nelson grasped her elbow.

"I'm not sure. Usually Tizzy sits outside, but the tent flaps are tied closed."

"You better read this, Ellen." Nelson pointed to an oil painting of Tizzy propped against the corner of the tent.

The artist had captured Tizzy in all her glory. Her dark eyes flashed and she wore her tribal robes, proudly displaying her brass-ringed neck. A copper tag had been glued to the bottom of the frame: Tizzy, Thai Queen. 1945-2005.

Heart aching, Ellen could feel her eyes welling with tears. When Nelson opened his arms, she went willingly and sniffled. "I decided to run away when I was twelve. Then I saw Tizzy and I asked if I could join the carnival and travel across the country with her."

"I wanted to run away once," Nelson commented.

Surprised, she asked, "How old were you?"

He chuckled. "Twenty-two. I had just graduated from college and didn't care to work for my grandfather's company."

"Why not?"

"Scared, I guess. Wasn't sure if I could handle the responsibility and live up to my grandfather's expectations."

"So why didn't you run away?"

"Too chicken to defy my grandfather." He curled his arm around her waist. "What did Tizzy say when you told her your plans?"

"She said families weren't perfect. And I shouldn't take my family for granted. She shamed me into feeling bad so I wouldn't even think about hurting them by running off."

"Tizzy was a smart woman."

"She was." After a longing glance at the portrait, they moved on, Ellen hating that the world around her constantly changed when *she* didn't. Yet, just because she chose to remain on the farm and do the same old thing day in and day out didn't mean the rest of the world had to follow suit.

How was it a young girl like Tizzy found the courage and strength to survive on her own and travel to a foreign land like America, while she, Ellen Tanner, lacked the guts to leave her own backyard? Pushing aside the depressing thought, she asked, "Ever been on a Ferris wheel?"

"No."

"Then it's about time. Besides, there's something I must discuss with you."

He motioned to the ride, visible over the tops of the tents. "You want to talk up there?"

Ellen studied his face. "You're afraid of heights, aren't you?"

"No," he insisted, but wouldn't make eye contact with her.

"I'll hold your hand," she offered, fighting a smile.

He frowned. "You think this is funny."

"No." She choked on the word, then lost the battle and laughed.

Clutching her hand, he headed for the ride. "You won't be laughing when I puke all over you."

"Eew!" She grimaced at the image.

The line for the ride was short. A good thing, considering Nelson appeared ready to bolt.

"You sure this ride is safe?" he asked.

"It worked okay the last time I rode on it."

"When was that?"

"Four years ago." She tapped the underside of his chin, and he snapped his mouth closed.

She attempted to view the ride through Nelson's eyes: peeling paint, rusty hinges and a few squeaky spokes. But no one fell out while they stood watching. That was a good sign.

When their turn to board arrived, Nelson stalled and she thought he'd chicken out. Then the ride operator asked, "You gettin' on or not, buddy?" Nelson lurched on to the seat.

As their feet left the ground, his knuckles whitened against the safety bar across their laps. *He really is afraid of heights.* Feeling terrible for badgering him, she set her pink cow in his lap and assured him, "Fuzzalina will keep you safe."

"Very funny."

Attempting to distract him, she pointed north. "There's the Klayton County courthouse."

"Uh-huh," he mumbled, his eyes shut so tightly his lashes had disappeared.

"If you want, the next time we pass the operator we can ask to get off."

"I'm fine. Now talk."

When she'd envisioned the conversation, Nelson hadn't had his eyes shut. "I wanted you to know I understand why you went to the bank on my behalf." She paused.

"Go on, I'm listening," he insisted.

"And…" She hesitated, fearing the words would

spill out in a jumble. "I realize it's been difficult for you to stand aside and watch me do things my way. You're a man used to controlling everyone and everything."

"You make me sound like a tyrant," he grumbled.

"Never a tyrant." She rested her hand over his white knuckles, and he surprised her by releasing the bar and threading his fingers through hers.

An image of his face while making love to her flashed through her mind. As he'd kissed her, he'd gazed into her eyes and she'd glimpsed the depth of his feelings for her. She was under no illusions he loved her. But she'd recognized deep caring.

It was this realization—he cared for her—that caused her to sympathize with his position. She applauded him for going against his natural instincts and permitting her to take the lead. Her admiration for him made her determined to meet him halfway.

Her conscience wouldn't allow Nelson to leave in September feeling guilty or worrying about her situation. If he pondered her at all from time to time, it would be of their lovemaking, and not the farm's dire financial situation.

It was the least she could do for him. He'd spun her head, flipped her heart and made her feel cherished—something she'd never experienced. "I've decided to accept a loan from you." *So I can hold on to you a little while longer.*

His eyes popped open. "Are you serious?"

She nodded, relieved the conversation had finally distracted him.

"Why the sudden change of heart?"

He had a right to be suspicious. But no way was she going to spill her guts. "None of your business."

Nelson snorted. "What's the catch?"

"Nothing."

"Then you'll accept my advice on how to use the money?" he persisted.

"I said I'd take your money, not your advice." The idea of running a larger operation didn't appeal to Ellen. Nor did selling. But Nelson was mistaken if he assumed his incessant lectures about the farm's financial troubles hadn't gotten through to her. She had a few ideas of her own on what to do with the money—the overdue Visa bill popped into her mind. And Seth.

No longer could she ignore the danger of not carrying health insurance for her or her son. When Buck had died, she'd had to cancel their health plan because she couldn't afford the monthly payment, never mind the obscene deductibles and office-visit co-pays.

Seth was her purpose in life, her one bright spot in an otherwise dull existence, and she was determined to do better by him. Even if she had to swallow her pride and accept a handout from Nelson.

And hopefully Nelson would feel an obligation to check up on her and his money periodically.

"A smart businessman learns what he's investing in before he doles out his cash."

"Sorry. You'll have to trust I know what's best for Seth, the farm and me. If you'd like to withdraw your offer..."

"Absolutely not."

"Okay, then. How much interest did you have in mind?" She considered pointing out the Ferris wheel had circled twice and his eyes had remained open the entire way, but decided against it.

"I'm not going to charge you interest."

"Then I'll have to refuse the loan."

"Wait a darn minute, Ellen. You can't—"

She rocked the seat.

"Whoa!" He clutched the bar and the color drained from his face. "Quit that."

"What's the interest rate?"

"Ellen, don't be stubborn about this."

Guilt prodded her, but she refused to back off. Pride could be nasty at times. She rocked the seat again, and Nelson's face went from white to green.

"Okay, okay. Stop. How's a half percent sound?"

"Ridiculous."

She reached for the safety bar.

"Wait!" he shouted. "Two percent."

"Five percent." When he hesitated, she warned, "Take it or leave it."

"Fine. Five percent," he groaned.

The ride ended. Luckily, they were the second couple off. Tossing Fuzzalina her way, Nelson bolted off the seat, stumbled to a garbage barrel and heaved.

Oh, dear Lord. She rummaged through her fanny pack for a tissue. "I didn't realize you were *that* afraid of heights."

He wiped his mouth, then glared. "I told you I was."

She wasn't sure if she was angry with herself for being mean or angry with Nelson for being stubborn.

Planting her hands on her hips, she demanded, "Then why in the world did you go on the Ferris wheel in the first place?"

"I went up on the damn thing because I wanted to make you happy," he grumbled.

Blast the man! His image blurred before her eyes. *This can't be happening.* She wasn't supposed to fall in love with him.

"Oh, hell. I didn't intend for the loan to make you cry," Nelson insisted, tugging her into his arms. "Whatever interest rate you choose is fine with me. Please stop crying."

He believed she was sobbing because of the loan? She bawled even harder.

"What's wrong with Mom?" Seth asked.

Startled by her son's voice, Ellen wiped the back of her hand across her eyes, sniffed and tried to calm herself.

"She was frightened. But she's fine now." Nelson wrapped an arm around her waist and tucked her against his side.

"Scared? Of what?" Brad asked.

"The Ferris wheel," Nelson explained.

Ellen buried her face against Nelson's chest and smiled.

"Mom's not afraid of the Ferris wheel. Did it break or something?"

Her chest shook with the struggle to hold in her laughter.

"Something like that," Nelson grumbled, then pinched her side. "I'm thirsty. You boys eat lunch yet?"

"No, sir," Brad admitted.

"We, um, spent our lunch money on games," Seth confessed.

Ellen shifted in Nelson's hold, aiming to scold the boys, but Nelson spoke first. "I could use a drink. Where would you guys like to eat?"

"There's a taco stand over there." Brad nodded to a greasy shack on the other side of the runway.

"Tacos it is. Let's go." Hand in hand, she and Nelson followed the boys. When she attempted to reclaim her hand, he gripped her fingers tighter. Too busy discussing shooting strategies for the basketball game they intended to play, neither Seth nor Brad paid them any attention.

When Ellen had decided to make love with Nelson, she hadn't considered how her relationship with him would affect Seth. She had no desire to flaunt anything in front of the boy and was positive Nelson would respect her wishes to keep their affair private. But now that she'd acknowledged she'd fallen head over heels for Nelson, it would be doubly difficult to hide her feelings from both Nelson and Seth.

Challenging or not, at the end of the summer, when Nelson returned to Chicago, she was determined that the only heart broken would be hers.

Chapter Twelve

"How often did your father bring you to Lake Culver?" Nelson asked Seth. He'd decided that while Ellen and Flo made pies for the upcoming church bake sale, he and the teen would spend Sunday afternoon playing Tom Sawyer and Huck Finn.

"Dad never took me fishing. But my grandpa drove me here when I was real little." Seth cast his line into the water, acting as if his father's lack of attention hadn't bothered him. Nelson suspected better.

The boy was starved for male attention. Since their trip to the Klayton County Fair three weeks ago, he'd made a concerted effort to spend more time with Ellen's son. After chores, they'd thrown the baseball, shot baskets at the hoop attached to the storage shed and played video games. As a result of the extra attention, Seth had opened up to Nelson.

Their conversations included typical guy stuff—cars, sports and computers. Then one afternoon the teen had confessed that he didn't understand why he missed his father, when the man had never spent any time with him. Without having considered the consequences, Nelson had hugged the boy. When Seth's skinny arms had squeezed back, a fragile bond had formed—a bond that troubled Nelson. How would Seth react when Nelson left the farm in five weeks?

Five weeks. The prospect depressed him. "Does your mom cook fish?"

"She fries 'em in batter."

"Then we'd better bring a few home for supper."

Seth grinned. "I bet I'll catch one before you do."

"Loser washes *and* dries the dishes," Nelson wagered, as he baited his hook.

"You're on." The boy reeled in his line, grabbed the tackle box and swaggered a few yards farther down the embankment, explaining, "So you don't steal my fish."

Nelson chuckled. After he and Seth settled into a companionable silence, he remembered thinking his first week on the farm had passed slower than a tugboat on the Mississippi. Each night he'd settled on the hard cot in the barn, the smell of cow manure pungent in the air, and he'd prayed he'd wake up the next morning and discover his life had all been a nightmare. Which of course hadn't been the case. Fanny Farmer, her cows and their odors had been as real as real could get.

Now, when he settled on the uncomfortable mattress, he wished he could roll back the hours. Days. The idea of never seeing Seth or Ellen after he left the farm made his chest physically ache—an ache the likes of which he'd never felt before. "Seth, you think you might want to visit me in Chicago sometime?"

"Heck, yeah." The teen's grin flipped upside down. "Mom can't leave the cows."

"I could always drive out to the farm and pick you up for a long weekend."

"Cool." Grin restored, the boy laid his pole on the ground, then rummaged through the tackle box.

Oh, hell. Why had Nelson raised Seth's hopes before conferring with his mother? He admitted his feelings for Ellen were complicated, tangled and confusing. And it wasn't because of the sex. Sex with Ellen had been incredible, exciting and emotional.

Sex aside, she'd come to mean *something* to him in the short time they'd been together. Regardless of what direction their relationship headed, he couldn't fathom permanently dropping out of her or Seth's life.

"If Mom won't let me see you, then I'll hitchhike to Chicago," the teen boasted.

Great. Ellen would blame him for enticing her son away from the farm with fascinating stories of life in the Windy City. "Thumbing rides is dangerous. If you really wish to see Chicago, I'll work something out with your mom."

"Promise?" Eyes as blue as his mother's begged.

Wincing, Nelson mumbled, "Promise."

They settled into an easy silence, affording Nelson the time to untangle his jumbled brain. If only he could figure out where he and Ellen stood as a couple. *He* considered them a couple, but wasn't sure Ellen did. The few times he'd hinted about the future, she'd changed the subject.

When he envisioned his life with no Ellen and no Seth, the picture wasn't pretty—it was gray, mundane and damn lonely. Could they survive a long-distance relationship if he returned to Chicago and she remained on the farm? His secretary had tried with an airline pilot and in the end the relationship hadn't survived the frequent separations.

He glanced sideways and his heart felt heavy when he considered never seeing what kind of man Seth would become. He cursed the farm that stood between Nelson and Ellen. He believed selling the place was in her best interest, but she seemed determined to go down with the ship. How could he save her when he wasn't positive she even cared to be rescued?

Although she'd never admitted it, Ellen had dropped enough hints that she wasn't truly happy living on the farm. But like many people in debt, she didn't have the means to change her circumstances. He wished he could convince her to set aside her pride and allow him to bankroll her. Not just a loan, but enough money to change her life.

With the financial resources to pay off her debts, he could offer her a chance to start over somewhere new. Do something with her life other than milk cows. If she sought to enroll in college or a trade school, he'd pay her tuition. And he'd make sure Seth received a good education and attended a university if he desired.

What about her argument that the farm is Seth's heritage? Not a problem. He'd buy the farm outright and hire a manager to run it, and even add improvements. Later, if Seth decided he'd like to return to his roots, he could. One way or another, he'd ensure Ellen ran out of excuses to stay in Four Corners. Then he'd give her a reason to start her life over—*him.*

He wanted to be the reason Ellen moved on with her life.

Maybe he was a fool to assume only the farm stood between him and Ellen. What about his career? If he could convince her to walk away from everything familiar, was he willing to rearrange his priorities? Willing to cut back on his work hours? Put her and Seth first in his life?

Part of him longed to. And part of him feared that once the excitement of their new life wore off, he'd revert to his old ways and get sucked back into the business again. And where would that leave Ellen? She was already a widow. She didn't deserve to become a divorcée.

"I caught something!" Seth shouted as his fishing pole bent toward the water.

Nelson dropped his pole and rushed to the teen's side. "Hold steady." When the pole slipped, Nelson grabbed it. After Seth regained control, he coaxed, "Slow and easy."

The boy's face reddened as he struggled to hold the pole with one hand while reeling in the fish with the other.

"The trout's at least a five-pounder," Nelson praised as the fish flopped about on the grassy bank.

"Wait till Mom sees this." Seth dropped to his knees and cut out the hook. "He sure is a fighter."

As Nelson watched the trout wiggle, he decided the fish and Ellen had a lot in common—neither one wished to give up.

"THAT'S THE FIFTH TIME you've stared off into space. What's wrong? You've been acting goofy all week," Flo insisted as she shoved a wad of napkins into a table dispenser.

Ellen continued stacking the water glasses, still warm from the dishwasher, under the lunch counter. Although they were alone in the diner, she debated confiding in her employer. But whom else could she talk to? Flo was the closest friend she had, even though twenty years separated them. Like a pig in a mud hole, she'd attempted to wade through the muck in her mind and hadn't gotten anywhere but stuck. *What the heck.* "I miss him."

Moving to the next table, Flo loaded another dispenser. "Miss who?"

"Never mind," Ellen mumbled, embarrassed she'd even considered spilling her guts about something so personal.

"Oh, no, you don't. I'm guessing the *him* you're missing is your hired hand?"

"Nelson." Just saying his name did funny things to Ellen's heart.

"When did he leave?" Flo asked.

"He hasn't left."

"I don't get it. How can you miss him if he's still hanging around your place?"

Ellen quirked an eyebrow, then a moment later watched her boss's lips form a perfect *O*.

Grabbing the broom and dustpan by the door, Flo proceeded to sweep under the tables. "So how far did you get with him?"

"What do you mean, how far?"

"Bases. You know, first, second, third."

Leave it to Flo to equate sex with baseball—her favorite sport. "We've, ah, crossed home plate…a few times," Ellen admitted, trying to ignore the heat crawling up her neck.

"And…" Flo grinned.

"And what?"

"And was it incredible?"

Incredible. Making love with Nelson went way beyond incredible. "Yes," she murmured, refusing to go into detail.

"I don't get it. If sex with him was so great, then why the hang-dog expression?"

Oh, shoot. She might as well spill her guts until her stomach was empty. "Nelson hasn't touched me lately. Not even a kiss. And I've given him plenty of opportunities."

Flo leaned on the broom handle. "Did you have a fight?"

"We don't fight. We *discuss.*"

"Okay, so what did you two *discuss?*"

Ellen shoved a strand of loose hair behind her ear. "It wasn't really a discussion—it was more of a look."

"Well, that's the first I've heard of a lookin' war," Flo grumped.

"I suspect he's upset with me because I didn't use the money he loaned me the way he'd hoped I would."

"It's about time you let someone help you." Her boss set the broom aside and untied her apron.

Not wanting to chat about the loan Nelson gave her,

she added, "Remember I told you he and Seth had gone fishing the day we baked pies for the church."

"Culver Lake, you said."

Ellen nodded. "When I returned home that afternoon, Nelson was…different."

Flo wiggled on to a stool at the lunch counter and lit a cigarette. "Different how?"

"It's as if he weighs each word before speaking. As if we're acquaintances, not lovers."

"Well, hell, Ellen. Just ask him what's bothering him."

"I can't." Because she was afraid he'd admit that she was nothing but a huge m-i-s-t-a-k-e.

"So you two haven't…played baseball since we baked pies?"

Ellen shook her head. "I've hinted, made sure I caught him alone in the barn so if he tried to kiss me he could. But…nothing."

"If I had a man like that at home, I'd be all over him like maple syrup on flapjacks." Flo checked her watch. "Go on, now. At least let me live vicariously through you. Because I'm sure as heck not getting anything."

"Elmer would be more than happy to oblige," Ellen teased as she grabbed her purse and keys from under the counter.

"Elmer's going to have to do a lot more wooing before I'll slip out of my skivvies for him."

"You're such a romantic, Flo."

"What's wrong with expecting flowers or a nice dinner—preferably somewhere other than a tavern?"

"Give him time. Elmer will come around," Ellen assured her, then left the diner, more determined than ever to confront Nelson.

SOMETHING WAS WRONG.

Nelson lay on his cot in the back room of the barn, holding his breath. He listened for a sound, a movement, anything to shatter the quiet darkness surrounding him.

There it was again—something stirred the air. The hair on his arms vibrated and his muscles tensed. Then...the faintest hint of lemon drifted beneath his nose.

Ellen.

He wasn't sure whether to exhale in relief or bounce off the mattress and scare twenty years off her life as she had his. Or maybe he'd feign sleep until he figured out for certain what the little farmer was up to, prowling around his room after midnight.

Forcing his eyes open, he studied the blackness. A shape hovered in the doorway. He didn't need to see or touch Ellen to recall her body. The silky patch of skin beneath her ear. The graceful lines of her neck. The gentle slope of her shoulders. The slight flair of her narrow hips. The sweet roundness of her bottom. The small fullness of her breasts. Two delicate pink nipples...

Her lemony scent grew stronger, her silent steps bringing her closer, increasing the ache in his loins.

All week, he'd struggled to keep his distance from her. He'd needed time to analyze his feelings. To be one-hundred-percent positive that what he felt for her was love. Ellen deserved nothing less from him. And he admitted he'd contracted a severe case of nerves each time he'd considered proposing.

Amazing… She hadn't laid a hand on him. Hadn't spoken a word. Yet she'd already won over his body and mind. Maybe the best way to show her his feelings was to make love to her. When she was sated and happy, he'd announce his intentions to spend the rest of his life with her.

In the darkness he held out his hand. Her breath hissed in surprise, then her shadow moved. A moment later her fingers glided across his palm. A gentle tug and she sat on the side of the cot. He cupped her face and brought her mouth to his.

Gentle, slow. The barest caress of lips. He ran his fingers along her arm, her skin as hot as his own. Her murmur registered in his brain, triggering a rush of testosterone to his groin.

He pulled her across his bare chest and assumed control of the kiss, thrusting his tongue inside her mouth. There would be no doubt in her mind how her midnight visit would end.

Ellen must have sensed his heightened desire. She slipped off her silky top, wiggled out of her pajama bottoms, then straddled his waist, arching her back, asking without words for more. He complied.

Caress after caress… Hands, mouths, moans and sighs filled the room until the air thickened with desire. Her touch grew bold straining his control, testing his limits. He tore his mouth from hers and shifted to his side, pinning her beneath him.

His wallet rested on the bedside table. However, the simple task of grabbing it became complicated when her teeth latched on to his nipple. He bucked against the sting of her bite, swearing beneath his breath. Husky laughter gurgled in her throat. He was in bed with a she-cat. He fumbled once more with the wallet, removed the condom and set it on the mattress. Her hands moved lower, pushing his boxers down his thighs. He twisted until they were around his ankles, then kicked them over the side of the cot. Her strokes grew bolder. Then her mouth replaced her hands and the beauty of her loving touched his soul.

Before he lost control, he shifted away from her hot caresses and muttered, "Your turn." He trailed kisses down her neck, over her breasts and across her belly, then between her thighs. He teased and tantalized until she begged him to free her.

He coaxed her up. One touch at a time. The darkness hid her face, but he imagined the blue of her eyes deepening to indigo as she gasped, then let loose a high-pitched moan as she climaxed.

When her breathing calmed, he cuddled her rump against his belly, then nestled his face in the crook of her neck. He breathed her in. Lost himself in her scent and her soft naked skin. A moment of panic seized him at the possibility this slip of a woman had the power to wrap a man his size around her little pinkie. And wrap him up, she did. Ellen had him tied in a knot only her deft fingers could unravel.

The minutes ticked by as they rested in silence. Not until Ellen's eager fingers moved behind her and stroked him did he remember he'd yet to find his own release. For a minute he allowed her roaming hands free reign over his body. Then she hooked her foot behind his calf and he decided to end his torment.

He sheathed himself, then gently entered her hot wetness. Her moans assured him she wasn't in any discomfort. When she rotated her head and offered her mouth, he feasted on it. His breath grew ragged. So did Ellen's. A moment later he felt her first tremor. At last he let go, his release thundering through him.

They must have dozed off, because Nelson awoke to light filtering through the open door. Ellen lay sprawled on top of his chest, her breasts smashed flat against him, her hair a tangled mass, covering half his face and neck. And her arms were locked around his waist as if she'd fallen asleep giving him a hug.

He brushed the strands of hair from her eyes. In sleep, she appeared too young to have a thirteen-year-old child. Too young to be running a farm by herself. Too young to have already lost a husband. A deep need to protect her filled him and he tightened his hold around her.

Soft, light-brown lashes fluttered, tickling his skin. She lifted her head. Her mouth curved and the tips of her white teeth peeked at him.

"Good morning," he mumbled.

Her smile widened. "Hungry?"

"For you, always."

The smile dimmed, catching him off guard. "What's wrong?"

A delicate shoulder shrugged. "You've been avoiding me all week."

"I'm sorry. I had a lot on my mind."

She plucked a hair on his chest and whispered, "Did you get it all figured out?"

"Yes." *I want to marry you.*

Ellen hadn't opened up about her relationship with her deceased husband, but Nelson sensed it hadn't been good. Would she even want to try marriage again? Maybe she'd prefer living together, instead. The concept of shacking up with her left a sour taste in his mouth. She deserved better and he didn't want to set a bad example for the boy.

But what if it didn't work out? What if after a while Ellen was unhappy living in the city? Would they return to their separate lives? Who would Seth live with? When would they see each other? His head pounded from all the questions. Right now, the one thing he was certain of was none of this would matter if Ellen didn't love him.

Never before had he stepped into a quagmire like this. Why did he have to go and fall in love with a woman like Ellen—attractive in a girl-next-door kind of way, stubborn, difficult, prideful, determined and so damn *alive. So perfect.*

Love. He rolled the word across his tongue again and again as he played with her silky hair. He was certain he loved her. But was his love strong enough to survive the ups and downs of marriage? Nelson thought of his brother, Ryan. His wife had run at the first sign of trouble and abandoned her husband when he'd needed her most.

Nelson searched his heart and knew he'd never leave Ellen—for any reason. He tilted her chin and gazed at her beautiful face. "I love you, Ellen."

Silence.

His lungs locked up. Had he mistaken her feelings for him? "You're making me nervous, Ellen. Say something."

Her big, blue eyes welled. With the pad of his thumb, he attempted to stem the tears leaking from the corners. Heart heavy, he choked, "I didn't mean to make you cry." He searched for the right words to ease her distress. "It's okay, angel. You don't have to say anything. I just needed you to realize how special you are to me." He kissed her, licking the salty tears pooling at the corners of her mouth.

She pulled away and sniffed, the tears continuing to flow. Only this time she smiled. "I love you, too, Nelson."

Her confession knocked the wind from his lungs. Relief, sharp and sweet, rushed through him. He hugged her, his heart lighter than it had been in days…months…maybe years. As long as Ellen loved him and he loved her, things would work out.

He wished they could snuggle in bed all morning and make plans for the future, but the *mooing* outside the barn grew louder. "We'll talk later. Right now Betty is having a cow."

She laughed at his corny joke and kissed him. Her lips, her mouth, her sighs telling him better than words how much she cared. The future looked bright, sunny and cheery.

Together they dressed, then strolled hand in hand from the barn.

Into the dark, blowing gusts of an oncoming storm.

Chapter Thirteen

Tornado.

"Lord help us." Ellen studied the mass of dark clouds swirling along the horizon. Mother Nature's ominous display was at the very least mesmerizing. The rotation at the bottom of the clouds guaranteed a twister was in the making. "We don't have much time."

"Tell me what to do," Nelson implored.

At the urgent note in his voice, she tore her attention from the sky. "Get Seth out of bed and turn off the gas and water in the house. Then head for the storm shelter. I'll let the cows loose into the pasture."

Instead of doing as instructed, Nelson grinned. *Grinned?* She demanded, "We're about to get our butts kicked by Mother Nature. Care to share what's so funny?"

He motioned to her body. "Are you planning to parade around in the storm wearing pajamas?"

She glanced at herself and cringed. "I'll grab a pair of coveralls in the barn."

Nelson snagged her arm, hauling her up against him. Stimulated by the rumble of thunder, the crackling lightning and their having made love only a short while ago, desire as powerful as the approaching tempest racked her body the moment his mouth covered hers. Hot, wet, possessive and edged with desperation, the kiss ended as abruptly as it had begun, leaving her gasping for air.

"Go," he urged.

Squinting against the dust particles stinging her face, she raced into the barn. After slipping on a pair of coveralls, she exited the side door into the holding area, where the small herd of cows huddled together. *They know.* She suspected the animals had sensed the storm hours before the clouds had appeared. The animals shifted nervously as she pushed her way between their hulking bodies. Once she opened the gate, the bovines scrambled for freedom.

Like a concerned mother, Betty hung back until the other cows had left, then sidled up and nudged her wet nose against Ellen's shoulder.

Ellen's throat closed as she drowned in Betty's big brown eyes. She and the cow had been through several bad storms over the past few years and had faired fine. No reason this storm would be any different. She threw her arms around Betty's massive neck and pressed her face to the warm, pungent hide. "Stay safe, my friend," she whispered, then patted her rump. The cow trotted after the others and Ellen secured the latch.

As if her feet had been nailed to the ground, she waited until the small herd disappeared over the swell in the terrain. If hearts could cry, then hers was bawling at the thought of her beloved cows unprotected in the open pasture. Tilting her face to the sky, she shook her fist at the turbulent heavens. "Damn you!" she ranted. A vicious gust of wind whipped the words back in her face. A sick feeling in her gut warned that this storm might be a killer. Time would tell how many victims it claimed after carving a wicked path of destruction through the area.

"Ellen!"

She whirled and spotted Nelson and Seth standing next to the storm cellar, motioning her to hurry. After one last, furious glance at the sky, she sprinted for cover. "Get inside!" she ordered.

"The key, Mom!" Seth pointed to the lock on the shelter door. "Where's the key?"

Panic squeezed her chest. She flung open the back porch screen door and frantically searched drawers and storage cabinets. They hadn't used the shelter since last summer, but that was a poor excuse for not remembering where she'd stowed the key. Why hadn't she thought to tape it to the wall above the door or to a window ledge? She checked behind the washer and dryer and under the welcome mat. Nothing. Her heart climbed higher in her throat. "I can't find it!" She left the porch, only to come to a screeching halt at the sight of Nelson hovering over the cellar, an ax poised high above his head.

Acting on instinct, she snagged Seth's T-shirt sleeve and yanked him behind her just as Nelson swung the ax down and severed the paddle lock with one mighty blow. He grasped the handle and jerked, but the wind caught the door, tearing it from his hold.

The rusty hinges snapped and the door sailed over their heads, slamming into the side of the house and shattering the kitchen window. Refusing to relinquish her death grip on her son's T-shirt, Ellen practically shoved Seth down the cellar steps.

Once their feet landed on the hard dirt floor, she guided him into the far corner. A shiver raced through her body—not from the cold damp air surrounding them but from fear. What if Nelson hadn't been here? Would she have managed to break the lock on her own? She shuddered at the vision of her and Seth being sucked into a funnel cloud.

Nelson joined them in the corner and wrapped his strong arms around her and Seth. The three of them raised their heads to the opening at the top of the stairs and watched in fascinated horror as pieces of debris flew past.

Although it was only six-thirty in the morning, the sliver of sky visible through the opening grew darker by the second and Ellen regretted not grabbing a flashlight from the back porch.

"Mom," Seth whimpered, squeezing her hand until it hurt.

"Everything will be okay, honey." *She prayed.*

"Sounds like a train passing through the yard." Nelson's breath fanned the top of her head.

Immediately following his comment, the wind died down and the dark sky turned a sickly green.

"Is it over, Mom?"

Lord, I wish. "We're in the eye," she whispered, afraid if the storm heard her it would increase its fury.

Nelson's hold tightened. "How long will we be stuck in the eye?"

"Depends on the size of the storm." *My poor cows.* She doubted they'd survive unscathed. Every vet within a hundred-mile radius would be busy for the next week tending to injured livestock. She kept a small supply of medicines and first-aid necessities for her animals in the barn…but the supplies would be gone if the barn blew away.

They waited in silence, her mind struggling to reconcile how one moment she'd gone from making love to Nelson and feeling on top of the world to being sucked into the underbelly of hell. The hairs on her nape quivered in warning. "Here it comes."

A clap of thunder shook the heavens, then a large tree limb sailed by the opening like a feather floating in the wind. *This is bad.*

She sent up a silent prayer for an end to the destruction. No sooner had she uttered amen than a large piece of metal debris, probably part of the barn, wedged itself in the opening, casting the shelter into pitch blackness.

"Stay calm," Nelson urged. "Chances are the wind will knock it loose."

Not five minutes later, the piece of metal shook and squeaked, and then a loud snap sounded as the debris popped free.

Big fat raindrops fell through the opening, wetting the stairs. "It's almost over."

"Are you sure, Mom?"

She was pretty sure it was the end of this storm. She

had no idea if another system was headed for them. She kissed Seth's mussed hair. "Rain and hail usually follow the eye."

Ping. Ping. Just as she'd predicted, hail—the size of small marbles—bounced down the cellar steps. Tears burned her eyes as she envisioned her cows out in the open, unprotected, hail pelting their hides. They waited for what felt like hours but was only a matter of minutes before the heavy rain abated and the hail let up.

"Stay here." Nelson climbed the stairs, then muttered, "I'll be damned" when he reached the top.

"What?" Ellen asked, poised on the bottom step.

"Half the sky is black. The other half is as blue as swimming-pool water." He made room for her when she reached his side. Seth wiggled between them.

"The barn's gone." Her son's voice cracked as he leaned into her.

Hugging him, she shivered and studied the remains of the structure—the cement slab and several steel support beams. Mangled pieces of metal were strewn across the driveway and adjoining acreage. Smaller debris was stuck in the tree. Two large limbs had been brutally severed from the trunk. One of the limbs lay across the truck bed, denting the metal. Her windshield had a spider crack running through it. The west side of her fence stood straight and tall. The east side had been blown flat, its posts scattered across the ground like toothpicks.

So much destruction…and she hadn't even inspected the house. She was afraid to turn around…afraid it wouldn't be there.

Nelson must have sensed her anxiety because he clasped her shoulder and assured her, "The house is still standing."

Sucking in a deep breath, she and Seth shifted as one to view the home behind them. Part of the roof had been torn off, but the walls remained intact. She envisioned the water damage inside and bit her lip to keep from bawling.

Nelson studied her face, then suggested, "Seth, let's check on my car."

Grateful Nelson sensed she needed a moment alone, she waited until the two males had disappeared around the corner of the house before she allowed her legs to buckle and she fell to her knees in the soggy grass. She couldn't stop the tears. Didn't even try to. She struggled to breathe, fearing she might hyperventilate.

Doomed. She was doomed. Her property insurance would cover some of the damage but not all. What did it matter? She couldn't afford the $20,000 deductible. Never mind replacing livestock. The pasture beyond the house wavered before her blurry eyes. Had any of her cows survived?

"Hey, Mom." Seth's excited voice carried to her from the front yard.

She scrubbed her eyes with grimy fingers and shouted, "Coming!" She forced her rubbery legs to support her.

When she rounded the corner of the house, Seth pointed to Nelson's car. "Look, Mom, only a few dents from the hail. Can you believe it?"

She stared in amazement. Aside from a few scratches, the vehicle appeared undamaged.

Nelson's happy grin pierced her heart. Despair filled her lungs, making it impossible to catch her breath. It wasn't fair. The tornado had destroyed her farm and left her home in shambles. Yet the same twister had spared Nelson's stupid little sports car. Despair gave way to anger. She dropped her gaze to the ground. When she spotted a rock the size of her fist, she picked it up and threw it as hard as she could at the car's windshield.

The damn stone bounced off the glass like a rubber ball. Stunned by her action, she stared in horror at Seth's and Nelson's shocked expressions. *Oh, God, I'm falling apart.*

Cautiously, Nelson approached, concern darkening his eyes. "You okay, Ellen?" he asked, gently touching her shoulder.

"Don't be nice to me. I did a terrible thing," she choked out.

"Come here, angel." He wrapped her in his arms and tucked her head beneath his chin. "Everything will be okay."

"No, it won't," she blubbered.

"Is Mom all right?" Seth's voice shook.

"She'll be fine, son." Nelson dug into his jeans pocket and removed his BlackBerry. "Phone Brad's family and find out if they're okay. Your mom and I are going out to locate the cows." Nelson set her from him, then wiped her face with his fingertips.

"Seth," she called as he walked away. "Stay here

in case the sheriff stops. And don't go into the house until we return."

Hand in hand, she and Nelson trekked through the pasture and beyond. Her first attempt to shout Betty's name ended in a warble. She hollered over and over, until her voice grew hoarse. It wasn't long before they happened upon a few of the cows.

Traumatized by the violent weather, they huddled together and were bawling softly. Ellen's quiet words and gentle caresses calmed them enough so she could inspect their condition. Aside from minor bruises and scratches, they appeared in good shape.

"Over here." Nelson waved to her from a clump of debris several yards away. "I'm sorry, Ellen." His sympathetic expression warned her as she approached the heap.

She recognized the solid black rump sticking out from the bottom of the pile. *Oh, Betty.* She dropped to her knees and began tossing aside pieces of wood, roof shingles, boards and other debris, heedless of the small nicks and scratches to her unprotected hands. When she'd finally uncovered the cow, she stopped breathing. An uprooted fence post had impaled the poor creature. Ellen rested her cheek against Betty's head. "Oh, sweetie. I'm so sorry." Tears poured from her eyes, soaking the cow's hide. Lost in her grief, Ellen was unaware of time passing and didn't utter a sound of protest when Nelson hauled her exhausted body into his arms and carried her back to the house.

Vulnerable.
Young.

So damn delicate.

Nelson stood next to the couch where Ellen napped...relaxed and worry-free. He checked his watch. After they'd returned from the gruesome discovery of Betty's carcass, he'd forced her to take a couple of pain-killers and lie down for a short while. Twelve hours had passed since she'd fallen into an exhausted sleep.

Seth had been able to contact Brad's family and Nelson had spoken with the father. Their property had suffered only minor damage and their house and barns had remained intact. Brad's father had suggested Seth spend a few days with them while Ellen came to grips with her situation, and the teen had jumped at the offer.

Obviously, Nelson's attempts to reassure the boy that everything would be fine had failed. Hell, the kid wasn't stupid. Seth understood the destruction from the tornado had left his mother in deep financial trouble.

While Ellen slept, Nelson had used the time to survey the damage to the house. Not only had the winds torn off the portion of roof that once covered the bedrooms, but it had damaged two of the outer walls, leaving the electrical wiring exposed. Upon closer inspection, he'd noticed the wiring was the outdated aluminum kind, not the standard copper used in homes today. Not only would Ellen have to replace the roof but she would also have to update the electrical wiring throughout the entire house. Add new barns, milking equipment, a vehicle, additional livestock, feed, fencing, supplies and a hundred other items necessary to run a dairy farm. Ellen had no choice now but to sell.

Her golden lashes fluttered and a moment later she opened her eyes. He sat on the edge of the sofa near her hip and brushed a knuckle across her cheek. "Good evening, sleepyhead."

Her mouth curved into a smile as she stretched her arms above her head, her back arching off the cushions. He recognized the instant she remembered the storm—her body stiffened and her smile vanished.

He pulled her into his arms and searched his brain for the words to help her feel better—but there weren't any. Helplessness—a feeling so foreign to him he hadn't a clue how to fight it—filled him. He tipped her chin. "Everything's going to be okay."

She shoved her palms against his chest, then swung her legs off the sofa, stood and swayed on her feet. "Easy for you to say when the storm didn't ruin your house or your barns or even your car."

Concerned about her physical well-being, he offered, "Let me get you something to eat."

Ignoring his offer, she asked, "Where's Seth?"

"He's staying at Brad's house for a couple of days. Their farm escaped the storm, but if you'd rather have him home, I'll drive over and get him."

"No. Let him be." She wrapped her arms around herself and shivered.

"I turned the water and gas back on. Why don't you soak in the tub while I make you a sandwich." Ellen needed to eat before she passed out.

"How long have I been asleep?" She gazed out the living-room window at the gathering shadows.

"Since early this morning."

"Why didn't you wake me?" Her chin trembled, but she bit her lip, refusing to cry.

Watching her struggle against tears was more than Nelson could bear. He reached for her, but she shied away, her rejection stinging more than he cared to admit. "Tomorrow is soon enough to begin cleaning up and making plans."

Cheeks pink with anger, she argued, "The cows should be fed and milked, then—"

"Ellen, stop." He consciously lowered his voice. "The cows will be fine. They can feed off the grass. After the scare they had today, they won't give milk for a while."

"The house has to be cleaned." She folded her arms over her chest and glared.

"No sense exhausting yourself for nothing."

"What do you mean, for nothing?"

She was in no shape, physically or emotionally, for this conversation, but she appeared determined to have it. "The storm was a sign, Ellen."

Eyes flashing, she snorted, "A sign?"

"I realize the farm means a lot to you, but it's gone. There's nothing left to keep you here." She opened her mouth, but he cut her off. "Let me finish."

Pacing the floor, he explained. "You maintained one of the reasons you stayed on the farm was Seth. You felt it was important to keep the dairy going in case he decided to take it over when he grew up." She looked ready to deny the charge, but she glanced away without uttering a word. "The dairy is gone, Ellen. The house has suffered major damage. The only thing left of value is the land."

"Are you suggesting I give up? Just walk off?"

"I wouldn't call it giving up. I could help you find a way to keep the land. If Seth wanted, he could return and rebuild when he's older."

"What if I don't care to quit?"

Nelson struggled to see past her I-don't-give-a-damn-what-you-think expression. "After all the destruction the storm caused, you're telling me you'd rather stay?"

"Insurance will pay for some of the repairs."

"True, but what about the deductible? How will you secure that kind of money?"

She crossed the room to the rolltop desk and rummaged through a drawer. After tossing aside papers, she removed a coffee can, popped the lid, then pulled out a wad of cash tied in a rubber band. "I have ten thousand dollars here."

Was she crazy? The money should be in a bank, not a desk drawer, where it could have been carried away by the tornado. Not sure how he felt about Ellen's stash, he asked, "How long have you had the money?"

She stared into space, her fingers clenching and unclenching the roll of bills. "I've been saving since before I got pregnant with Seth."

"Saving for what?" When she didn't answer, he repeated, "Ellen, why haven't you used the money to pay off your debts?"

After a never-ending minute she blurted, "To run away, okay?"

Run away?

Her mouth curved. "I yearned to run away to the

city. Then I got pregnant." Her shoulders slumped. "And married and well…" She shrugged. "I kept saving…in case."

Stunned by what she'd revealed, Nelson sat on the couch cushions. "Why are you still here, Ellen?" he badgered. She had to admit her fear before she could move on with her life. Before she could move on to *him.*

Turning her back, she spat, "It doesn't matter."

"From where I'm sitting, it matters a hell of a lot."

"Fine." She faced him. "You want an answer?"

His goal hadn't been to anger her, but anger was better than the misery shining in her eyes earlier.

"Dairy farming is all I do, Nelson. I have a son to support. I can't just run off and play at a new career."

"Maybe I'm confused. But I believe we were pretty damn honest with our feelings for each other before the storm hit."

She refused to make eye contact. "I have strong feelings for you, Nelson. I won't deny that."

Strong feelings? "You said you loved me." When she remained silent, he added, "I said I loved you."

"We were caught up in the—"

"No." He shot off the couch. "I love you, Ellen. I wish to make a life with you and Seth. I want us to get married. I want you both to move to Chicago. I want us to be a family."

"The farm—"

"There is no farm. The storm was a signal—a signal to move on with your life."

"I'm not ready to move on."

"What about Seth? Do you care about what he wants? Is it fair to make him suffer because you're afraid?"

"Seth doesn't mind the farm."

"That's a lie." He swept his arms out in front of him. "This isn't the life he wants, Ellen. Together, we can show him what the world has to offer besides cows." When she didn't speak, he added, "You're not being fair."

"This isn't about *fair.* This is about keeping a roof over our heads and food on the table."

"If you marry me, Ellen, you won't have to worry about those things."

He read the indecision in her eyes. Deep down in his gut he clung to the belief her love for him would make her see reason. But a full minute passed and only silence filled the room. His heart heavy, he searched for the right words to sway her. To make her accept that his love for her was all she needed to leave the only life she'd ever known.

Throat tight, he confessed, "After we made love the first time I realized you were the one, Ellen. *The one.*" He cleared his throat. "None of this stuff—the house, the barns, the cows—matters. What matters is here." He thumped his chest with his fist. "You know why?"

She bit her bottom lip and shook her head.

"Because together we can overcome your fear."

"You're talking crazy," she protested.

He waited. Hoped. Prayed she'd give him a reason to believe they had a chance. Each second that passed in silence felt like a dagger in his heart. "You're a strong woman, Ellen Tanner. In the short time we've been together I never once expected you'd let your fears deny you or your son happiness." He moved to the door. "I guess I was wrong."

"Where are you going?" Her voice wobbled.

His hand shook over the knob. "Back to Chicago."

"But you agreed to work for me until Labor Day."

"I can't, Ellen. I can't stay and watch you throw your life away on this farm." *I can't stay and fall more in love with you every day, knowing you won't let us be together.*

"Wait a cotton-pickin' minute. What about this acquiescence lesson your grandfather expects you to learn? You're supposed to be taking orders from me, remember?"

Nelson closed his eyes when he heard the catch in her voice, but didn't attempt to defend himself.

"I'm the boss here, damn it. And I'm ordering you to stay."

His heart went numb. The sooner he escaped, the better. He removed his BlackBerry and the charger from his pocket and tossed them across the room, where they landed on the sofa next to the pink cow he'd won her at the fair. "Use that until they restore your phone service. And don't worry about cleaning up the debris. I'll handle everything."

"Nelson!"

Heart threatening to split in two, he walked out the door and stumbled to his car, the sour taste of defeat gagging him.

Chapter Fourteen

Shoulder propped against the wall, Nelson studied the flying angels etched in the stained-glass windows along the church corridor. St. Patrick's sat in the heart of Santa Angelita, a small Los Angeles barrio where his brother Aaron planned to marry his former construction boss, Jennifer Alvarado, in—Nelson checked his watch—less than thirty minutes.

Yesterday, Aaron had taken Nelson on a tour of the barrio, and he had to admit, he'd been impressed with his brother's vision for the small neighborhood nestled in South Central L.A. After viewing his latest urban-renewal project, a renovated canning factory converted into affordable condos, Nelson believed Aaron had found his true calling. Not only had he created a rewarding and fulfilling job for himself within the McKade family empire, but it was obvious by the way local residents treated and respected him that he'd been embraced by the mostly Latino community.

Yep, life was good for Aaron—making one of the three McKade brothers happy. Attempting to loosen the noose around his neck, Nelson tugged at his pre-tied bow tie. The tux didn't fit well—par for the course. Nothing in his life *fit* anymore.

He blamed his unsettled emotions on the cute little farmer he'd left behind in Four Corners, Illinois, three weeks ago. He'd driven away from Ellen's farm with a hole in his heart the size of his fist. During the trip home he'd decided he was through with women. He'd intended to live the rest of his life alone. To wallow in self-pity and misery for the next fifty years or more, considering longevity ran in his family. With his luck, he'd live to be the age of his grandfather, who at 91 had danced a mean jitterbug at the rehearsal dinner.

Nelson had planned out the rest of his miserable existence, but after a few days had passed he'd admitted that he couldn't—wouldn't—let Ellen slip away without a fight.

"Hiding?" Ryan McKade taunted, straightening his own bow tie as he walked down the hallway.

"Yes." Nelson studied his brother's carefully blank expression. A casual observer might mistake Ryan for a serious man. Nelson knew better. As a result of 9/11, a haunted emptiness had taken up permanent residence in his brother's eyes.

Pretending interest in one of the stained-glassed windows, Ryan murmured, "Nice day for a wedding."

No doubt Aaron's nuptials brought back memories of Ryan's wedding to his ex ten years earlier. The fact that Aaron's wife-to-be was already expecting their first child no doubt increased Ryan's misery. Nelson searched his mind for something to say. Since the at-

tack on the World Trade Center, his brother had erected
a barrier around himself that not even his family had
been able to break through.

Ryan ended the awkward silence. "I hear you've
changed your management style. Looks like your lesson in acquiescence has paid off."

Ignoring his brother's smirk, Nelson admitted,
"You could say I'm delegating now." He'd formed
teams, and within the company had handed over many
of the decision-making responsibilities to the men
and women in charge of the groups. Stepping aside
while others formulated business strategies had been
difficult but necessary, considering how determined
he was to marry Ellen.

His staff's increased enthusiasm and productivity
had made him grudgingly admit his grandfather's
crazy *life lesson* hadn't been so crazy after all. More
important, if he hadn't agreed to appease his grandfather, he would never have met Ellen.

"So you're content to be back in the office?"

The question interrupted Nelson's musings. "Yes…"
He expelled a frustrated breath, then shoved a hand
through his neatly combed hair. "No, damn it, I'm not."
He wanted to be with Ellen, even if it meant milking a
bunch of stupid cows for the rest of his life.

With eyes wiser than his years, Ryan asked, "You
fell in love with her, didn't you?"

"Is it that obvious?" Nelson grumped.

A wry smile tilted the corner of Ryan's mouth. "Does
she love you?"

"I think so."

"You think so?"

Embarrassed his emotions were in a state of chaos, Nelson mumbled, "It's complicated."

His brother laughed, the sound tainted with bitterness.

"Ellen's confused and frightened. I believe she loves me—but I'm not sure love is enough to make her leave the farm." Nelson conceded her inability to trust him—trust in their love for each other—had cut deep.

"Call her," Ryan suggested. When Nelson remained silent, he chuckled. "You always had too much pride."

Pride—no. Fear—yes. As long as he didn't confront Ellen, he could cling to the belief everything would work out between them—not a very mature way to handle the situation. "I left my BlackBerry with her. But she hasn't phoned."

The night he'd fled the farm, he'd stopped for gas halfway to Chicago. He'd sat in the car and stared at a payphone, his hands choking the steering wheel until pain shot through his knuckles. The urge to return to the farm and beg her to give him—them—a second chance had almost made his stomach revolt. Maybe it had been stubborn pride or plain frustrated anger, but he'd convinced himself they'd both needed time to think things through. He'd been positive with a little breathing room, Ellen would realize they were meant to be together.

Back in Chicago, he'd waited for her phone call. He didn't have his home number listed in the Black-

Berry, but his office number and his grandfather's were. One day had passed. Another. And another. Then a week. Here it was the third Saturday in August and still no word from Ellen.

"If I wasn't witnessing it with my own eyes, I would never have believed a woman could make you this miserable, big brother."

"Very funny."

Ryan's expression sobered. "Call her, Nelson."

"What if she doesn't—" He snapped his mouth closed, unable to voice his worry. He was behaving like a moron. That a pint-sized farmer had him running scared confounded him. Always the one in control of everything, the realization he was human and vulnerable scared him.

"I'd have never guessed you were such a coward."

Coward? Nelson noticed the pink tinge crawling up his brother's neck. He could have easily tossed the insult right back in Ryan's face, but didn't have the heart. Instead, he removed his new BlackBerry from the breast pocket of his tux and punched in the farm's number. If Ellen didn't want to talk to him, fine. He'd do all the talking.

After two rings, a recorded message announced that her number had been disconnected. *Disconnected?* Panic gripped his gut. The telephone company should have restored service by now. Praying she hadn't tossed the device into the garbage, he dialed its number and got his voice mail.

His heart crawled into his throat. "She's not answering."

"Then go after her," Ryan encouraged.

"Never thought my big brother would be tied up in knots over a woman."

Nelson recognized his brother Aaron's voice. Aaron and his soon-to-be-wife, Jennifer, stood at the end of the corridor.

"Don't you know it's bad luck to see the bride before the wedding?" Nelson shifted from one foot to the other, feeling hemmed in by his two brothers.

Aaron grabbed Jennifer's hand and moved forward until the four of them created a cozy family circle. "We've been searching for you guys. The wedding begins in five minutes."

Oh, hell. "I'm sorry." Nelson offered his apology to the bride. He made a move to head to the church sanctuary, but Jennifer snagged his jacket sleeve.

"Nelson." She glanced sideways at Aaron, then urged, "Don't wait another minute. Go after her right now."

"We're about to get married, Jenny!" Aaron protested.

The intimate smile the bride bestowed upon her groom turned the grown man to mush before Nelson's eyes. "I know." She caressed Aaron's cheek, and the love shining in her eyes was so brilliant it almost blinded Nelson, and made him ache to hold Ellen in his arms.

"I was so sad after I ran you off, Aaron. I've always regretted that I never went after you. I made both of us miserable far longer than we deserved." She leaned into Aaron, pressing against his side, and urged, "Let him go after her. Please."

Aaron's besotted expression said he'd do anything to make his wife-to-be happy.

Turning to Nelson, Aaron grumped, "Get out of here. Go find your Ellen."

"What about Grandfather?" Nelson asked. "He's already miffed at me for cutting my life lesson short."

"Has he told you he's scratched your name from his will?" Ryan asked.

"No, not yet." Though Nelson half expected him to. Strangely enough, he didn't care. Didn't care because his happiness wasn't tied to money anymore. It was tied to Ellen and Seth. And the three of them being a family.

"Then as long as you don't run off to Vegas to get married, he'll forgive you for skipping out on our wedding," Aaron assured him.

Grinning, Nelson hugged both brothers and kissed the bride's cheek. "Thanks for understanding." Then he vanished out a door leading to the parking lot behind the church.

Aaron grinned at Ryan. "Two down, one to go."

GRIPPING THE steering wheel tighter, Nelson took the exit off the highway that led to Four Corners. The trip had taken less time than he'd anticipated, no doubt due to the fact that he hadn't encountered a herd of pigs along the way.

Forty-eight hours had passed since he'd cut out on his brother's wedding. He'd caught the first plane from L.A. to Chicago, but the normal three-and-a-half-hour flight had taken twelve. An equipment failure had grounded the plane for two hours. After takeoff, another malfunction had forced the pilot to land in Phoenix. There, Nelson and the other passengers sat in the terminal for five hours until the plane had been given clearance to continue its flight to Chicago.

As soon as he'd landed at O'Hare, he'd caught a cab to his apartment, thrown a handful of clothes into a duffel bag, grabbed a quick shower and hit the road at dawn. He glanced at the dashboard clock—7:30 a.m. He should be dead on his feet. Instead, he felt energized, excited and eager to reach his destination— Ellen. And he admitted the two, triple-shot espressos from Starbucks he'd grabbed on the way out of town had kept him alert behind the wheel.

On the outskirts of Four Corners, he veered right on to the county road leading to the farm. Signs of the recent tornado remained—downed tree limbs, debris, garbage clogging the ditches and a billboard severed in half. Another mile and the backside of Ellen's property came into view.

He pulled on to the shoulder in front of the farm and shifted the car into Park. A steel chain securing the front gate prevented entry. Puzzled, he left the car. He'd hired a company to clear the wreckage from the property and they appeared to have done a decent job. Then he spotted the blue tarp covering the roof of the house and frowned. Why hadn't the men put on a new roof yet? He glanced sideways and noticed a sign nailed to the fence.

Sold.

What? No one was home—Ellen's truck was gone—but he shouted anyway. "Ellen! Seth!"

His previous state of euphoria took a nosedive, leaving him shaky and unsteady. *Flo.* He hustled back to the car. Flo would tell him where Ellen had gone. As he sped toward town, the fear in his gut gave way to anger. Better anger than fear. Ellen should have informed him she'd put the farm up for sale. He deserved at least that small courtesy after his attempts to save the place. He suspected her neighbor had purchased the property—probably got it for a steal.

When Nelson arrived in Four Corners, several vehicles sat outside the diner. He ended up having to park the Jaguar across the street. He entered the diner and all heads swiveled his way. He ignored the attention, searching for Flo in the breakfast crowd.

"Howdy, stranger," she greeted him, balancing two plates of steaming eggs and fried potatoes. "Be right with ya." She delivered the food to a couple across the room, then socialized for a minute before returning to Nelson. "What brings you back to Four Corners?"

Exchanging pleasantries was the last thing on his mind. "Where's Ellen?"

Flo's smile froze.

"I saw the *sold* sign. When did she leave? Where did she go?"

The frozen smile thawed. Frowning, Flo insisted, "Off to start a new life."

A new life without him? Not if he had any say in the matter. "This is important. I have to talk to her."

The older woman adopted the female battle stance—fists planted on her hips. Chin high. Chest out. "Why?"

Sensing the diner owner wouldn't budge unless he told the truth, Nelson confessed, "I love Ellen. And I want to marry her."

Eyes narrowed, Flo asked, "What if Ellen wants to continue dairy farming?"

"I'll milk cows for the rest of my life if it means I can be with Ellen."

"And Seth?"

"I'll be a good father to him." He sensed her softening, but just in case, he added, "Please, Flo."

"She made me pinkie-swear not to say anything."

"At least tell me when she left town."

"A few minutes ago."

Nelson couldn't believe his luck. He'd figured Ellen had a three-week jump on him.

"Which direction did she head?"

"That way." A pink fingernail pointed east. The direction Nelson had come from. He hadn't noticed her truck on the way to the diner, so he assumed she passed the turnoff to the farm a few minutes before he'd reached the country road.

"Thanks, Flo." He grabbed her around the middle, lifted her and hugged her.

"Oh, for Pete's sake, put me down." She pummeled his back with her fist. When he set her on her feet, she warned, "You better not hurt her, Nelson. She deserves a happily-ever-after."

"I intend to see she gets one." He grinned. "We'll invite you to the wedding."

"Go on, now. You've wasted enough time jabbering."

Nelson rushed to his car and sped out of town. Ellen couldn't have gotten too far. His gut clenched when he envisioned her and Seth traveling alone in a truck that should have found its way to the salvage yard ten years ago.

After several minutes he spotted a vehicle parked on the shoulder. As he drew nearer there was no mistaking the rusted rattletrap—Ellen's truck. He eased his car on to the shoulder several yards behind the battered Ford. At first he didn't spot Ellen or Seth, and worried they'd hitched a ride to town with a stranger.

When he exited the car, the sound of arguing met his ears and he grinned. Ellen and her son had their heads stuffed under the raised hood. He snuck up on them.

"The oil's leaking, Mom," Seth argued.

"No. It's a plug."

"What do you know about plugs? Check the dipstick," Seth insisted.

"Engine trouble?" Nelson asked.

At the sound of his voice, Ellen squawked and jumped a foot in the air.

Seth grinned. "Hey, Mr. McKade. Perfect timing. The truck's busted."

"Looks to be," he answered, then turned his attention to the woman who'd made his life miserable for the past few weeks.

Sporting pigtails, she wore a sunny yellow T-shirt, overalls and white canvas tennis shoes. Man, how he'd missed his little farmer. She might appear as delicate as a flower, but Nelson acknowledged the magnitude of strength and grit in her petite body. She was his equal in every way.

If his insides weren't shaking, he'd scold her for risking her and Seth's safety by taking off in a rundown truck. But right now all he could manage was, "I've missed you, Ellen." He stroked his fingertip across the bridge of her nose. He'd even missed her freckles.

Shifting from one foot to the other, Ellen confessed, "Nelson, there's something I have to tell you."

Couldn't they just kiss first?

"Aw, man. If you guys are gonna talk, can I sit in your car and listen to the radio, Mr. McKade?" Seth asked.

"Sure. Keys are in the ignition." As soon as the teen got comfortable in the driver's seat and blasted the music, Nelson said, "I need to tell *you* something."

"Me first, Nelson." She drew in a deep breath. "I was afraid...scared to death." Her voice broke, reminding him of an injured animal's.

"Ah, angel, I know you were afraid to leave the farm. But—"

"It was more than that." She rolled a pebble beneath her shoe. "For a long time I'd convinced myself I didn't have the skills or knowledge to do anything else but milk cows." She raised her head, allowing him a glimpse of her soul. "Then you arrived and I fell in love with you and—" she sniffed "—I was forced to admit my real fear."

"Your real fear?"

"That I'm not good enough."

"Good enough for what?"

"For you, Nelson."

"Where the hell did you get that idea? I proposed to you, didn't I? I said I loved you. I never—"

"Shh." She touched his arm. "You never once made me feel inferior, Nelson. But in here—" she touched her palm to her heart "—I believed I wasn't an exciting enough woman for you. Wasn't pretty enough. Educated enough. Sophisticated enough. I was sure that after the newness of sleeping with me wore off, you'd move on."

"He really did a job on you, didn't he?" Nelson's gut burned with anger at her deceased husband.

Her eyes teared. "I've never told anyone this, but Buck asked me for a divorce a week before he died."

"I'm sorry, angel." He gathered her into his arms.

"Buck said I was uninspiring. A rock around his neck." She clasped Nelson's face between her hands. "Until you, I hadn't realized I'd lost the most important thing."

"What did you lose, Ellen?" he whispered. *I promise we won't stop looking until we find it.*

"My self-esteem." She poked a finger in her chest. "I was so angry and hurt when you walked out after the storm. I bawled my head off for hours."

An image of Ellen, face buried in a pillow, sobbing, flashed before Nelson's eyes and he cringed.

"But you leaving was the best thing that could have happened to me."

Confused, he asked, "How?"

"I took a long gander in the mirror and…I was

ashamed at the coward that stared back at me." She gave herself another poke. "I believe I deserve better from life than what I've allowed myself and my son to have. Seth should have a chance to reach for his own dreams." She lifted her chin. "But I don't intend to be a burden to you."

"You'll never be a burden. And just for the record, Ellen, you inspire the hell out of me. You made me realize that while I thought I was living life to the fullest by devoting every waking hour to the business, I was, instead, letting life pass me by."

"Oh, Nelson. I have so many dreams"

"Do I figure into any of them?"

Her smile rivaled the sun. "Yes."

"Then why are you running away from me?"

"Nelson, which direction is the truck pointing?"

"East." What did that have to do with anything?

She slipped her arms around his waist. "I'm not running from you. I'm running to you."

When Ellen's words sank in, Nelson's breath left his lungs in one huge gust of air. He buried his face in her neck, afraid to speak for fear his voice would break.

"I love you with all my heart, Nelson."

Cupping her face, he searched her eyes. "I promise to help you reach your dreams."

"I'm glad, because here's my biggest dream of all." She clasped both his hands in hers. "Nelson McKade, will you marry me and be the kind of father Seth deserves?"

Throat tight with emotion, he assured her, "I'd be honored to marry you, Ellen. There's nothing that would make me happier than to be your husband and Seth's father."

"Are you guys gonna get all mushy and stuff?" Seth hollered, his head hanging out the driver's side window.

"Yes!" Ellen and Nelson shouted in unison.

The teen stuck his finger in his mouth and made a gagging sound, then slouched in the seat until only the top of his head remained visible.

"I'm going to make sure we have an adults-only honeymoon," Nelson grumbled before capturing Ellen's mouth. He brushed his lips across hers, reacquainting himself with the soft flesh before tasting the sweetness inside. He could have kissed her forever, but she wiggled loose from his hold and told him, "I'll grab my purse from the truck while you load our luggage in your car."

Nelson grinned like a buffoon.

Acquiescence wasn't such a bad thing if Ellen Tanner-McKade was the woman he had to take orders from the rest of his life.

* * * * *

Happily ever after is just the beginning…

Turn the page for a sneak preview of
DANCING ON SUNDAY AFTERNOONS
by
Linda Cardillo

Harlequin Everlasting—Every great love
has a story to tell.™
A brand-new line from Harlequin Books
launching this February!

Prologue

Giulia D'Orazio
1983

I had two husbands—Paolo and Salvatore.

Salvatore and I were married for thirty-two years. I still live in the house he bought for us; I still sleep in our bed. All around me are the signs of our life together. My bedroom window looks out over the garden he planted. In the middle of the city, he coaxed tomatoes, peppers, zucchini—even grapes for his wine—out of the ground. On weekends, he used to drive up to his cousin's farm in Waterbury and bring back manure. In the winter, he wrapped the peach tree and the fig tree with rags and black rubber hoses against the cold, his massive, coarse hands gentling those trees as if they were his fragile-skinned babies. My neighbor, Dominic Grazza, does that for me now. My boys have no time for the garden.

In the front of the house, Salvatore planted roses. The roses I take care of myself. They are giant, cream-colored, fragrant. In the afternoons, I like to sit out on the porch with my coffee, protected from the eyes of the neighborhood by that curtain of flowers.

Salvatore died in this house thirty-five years ago. In the last months, he lay on the sofa in the parlor so he could be in the middle of everything. Except for the two oldest boys, all the children were still at home and we ate together every evening. Salvatore could see the dining room table from the sofa, and he could hear everything that was said. "I'm not dead, yet," he told me. "I want to know what's going on."

When my first grandchild, Cara, was born, we brought her to him, and he held her on his chest, stroking her tiny head. Sometimes they fell asleep together.

Over on the radiator cover in the corner of the parlor is the portrait Salvatore and I had taken on our twenty-fifth anniversary. This brooch I'm wearing today, with the diamonds—I'm wearing it in the photograph also—Salvatore gave it to me that day. Upstairs on my dresser is a jewelry box filled with necklaces and bracelets and earrings. All from Salvatore.

I am surrounded by the things Salvatore gave me, or did for me. But, God forgive me, as I lie alone now in my bed, it is Paolo I remember.

Paolo left me nothing. Nothing, that is, that my family, especially my sisters, thought had any value. No house. No diamonds. Not even a photograph.

But after he was gone, and I could catch my breath from the pain, I knew that I still had something. In the middle of the night, I sat alone and held them in my hands, reading the words over and over until I heard his voice in my head. I had Paolo's letters.

* * * * *

Be sure to look for
DANCING ON SUNDAY AFTERNOONS
available January 30, 2007.
And look, too, for our other
Everlasting title available,
FALL FROM GRACE by Kristi Gold.

FALL FROM GRACE is a deeply emotional story
of what a long-term love really means. As Jack
and Anne Morgan discover, marriage vows
can be broken—but they can be mended, too.
And the memories of their marriage have an
unexpected power to bring back a love
that never really left....

This February...

Catch NASCAR Superstar **Carl Edwards** *in*
SPEED DATING!

Kendall assesses risk for a living—
so she's the last person you'd
expect to see on the arm of a
race-car driver who thrives on the
unpredictable. But when a bizarre
turn of events—and NASCAR
hotshot Dylan Hargreave—inspire
her to trade in her ever-so-structured
existence for "life in the fast lane"
she starts to feel she might be
on to something!

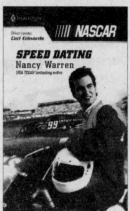

Collect all 4 debut novels in the Harlequin NASCAR series.

SPEED DATING
by *USA TODAY* bestselling author
Nancy Warren

THUNDERSTRUCK
by Roxanne St. Claire

HEARTS UNDER CAUTION
by Gina Wilkins

DANGER ZONE
by Debra Webb

On sale February 2007

What a month!

In February watch for

Rancher and Protector

Part of the Western Weddings miniseries

BY JUDY CHRISTENBERRY

The Boss's Pregnancy Proposal

BY RAYE MORGAN

Also in February, expect
MORE of what you love
as the Harlequin Romance line
increases to six titles per month.

HARLEQUIN *Presents*

Welcome back to the exotic land of Zuran, a beautiful
romantic place where anything is possible.

**Experience a night of passion
under a desert moon in**

Arabian Nights

Spent at the sheikh's pleasure...

Drax, Sheikh of Dhurahn, must find a bride for his brother—
and who better than virginal Englishwoman Sadie Murray?
But while she's in his power, he'll test her wife-worthiness
at every opportunity....

TAKEN BY
THE SHEIKH
by Penny Jordan

Available this February.
Don't miss out on your chance to own it today!

REQUEST YOUR FREE BOOKS!
2 FREE NOVELS PLUS 2
FREE GIFTS!

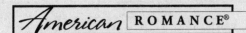

Heart, Home & Happiness!

YES! Please send me 2 FREE Harlequin American Romance® novels and my 2 FREE gifts. After receiving them, if I don't wish to receive any more books, I can return the shipping statement marked "cancel." If I don't cancel, I will receive 4 brand-new novels every month and be billed just $4.24 per book in the U.S., or $4.99 per book in Canada, plus 25¢ shipping and handling per book and applicable taxes, if any*. That's a savings of close to 15% off the cover price! I understand that accepting the 2 free books and gifts places me under no obligation to buy anything. I can always return a shipment and cancel at any time. Even if I never buy another book from Harlequin, the two free books and gifts are mine to keep forever.

154 HDN EEZK   354 HDN EEZV

Name _____ (PLEASE PRINT)

Address _____ Apt. #

City _____ State/Prov. _____ Zip/Postal Code

Signature (if under 18, a parent or guardian must sign)

Mail to the **Harlequin Reader Service®**:
IN U.S.A.: P.O. Box 1867, Buffalo, NY 14240-1867
IN CANADA: P.O. Box 609, Fort Erie, Ontario L2A 5X3

Not valid to current Harlequin American Romance subscribers.

Want to try two free books from another line?
Call 1-800-873-8635 or visit www.morefreebooks.com.

* Terms and prices subject to change without notice. NY residents add applicable sales tax. Canadian residents will be charged applicable provincial taxes and GST. This offer is limited to one order per household. All orders subject to approval. Credit or debit balances in a customer's account(s) may be offset by any other outstanding balance owed by or to the customer. Please allow 4 to 6 weeks for delivery.

Your Privacy: Harlequin is committed to protecting your privacy. Our Privacy Policy is available online at www.eHarlequin.com or upon request from the Reader Service. From time to time we make our lists of customers available to reputable firms who may have a product or service of interest to you. If you would prefer we not share your name and address, please check here. ☐

HAR07

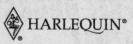

HARLEQUIN®

American ROMANCE®

COMING NEXT MONTH

#1149 THE DOCTOR'S LITTLE SECRET by Jacqueline Diamond
Fatherhood
Dr. Russ McKenzie doesn't have much in common with shoot-from-the-hip
policewoman Rachel Byers. Nevertheless, he shares his little secret with her.
Soon the two of them could be keeping it for life!

#1150 HER PERFECT HERO by Kara Lennox
Firehouse 59
The firefighters of Firehouse 59 are stunned when Julie Polk decides to convert
a local hangout into a *tearoom!* Determined not to let that happen, they elect
resident Casanova Tony Veracruz to sweet-talk the blonde into changing her mind.
But when Tony wants more than just a fling with Julie, he's not sure where his
loyalties lie....

#1151 ONCE A COWBOY by Linda Warren
Brodie Hayes is a former rodeo star, now a rancher—a cowboy through and
through. Yet when he finds out some shocking news about the circumstances
of his birth, he begins to question his identity. Luckily, private investigator
Alexandra Donovan is there to help him find the truth—but will it really
change who he is?

#1152 THE SHERIFF'S SECOND CHANCE by Leandra Logan
When Ethan Taggert, sheriff of Maple Junction, Wisconsin, hears
Kelsey Graham is coming home for the first time in ten years, he wants to
be there when she arrives. Not only is he eagerly anticipating seeing his former
crush, he's also there to protect her. After all, there's a reason she couldn't
return home before now....

www.eHarlequin.com